TWENTY OF TODAY'S BEST
SHORT STORIES

TWENTY OF TODAY'S BEST SHORT STORIES

AN ANTHOLOGY
By Some Of Today's
Finest Authors

Commonwealth Books Inc.,

CONTENTS

Published by Commonwealth Books Inc.,

Copyright © 2021 by Commonwealth Books

ISBN: 978-1-892986-23-8

Library of Congress Control Number: 2021930998

www.commonwealthbooks@aol.com

www.commonwealthbooksinc.com

Manufactured in the United States of America

CONTENTS

TWENTY OF

TODAY'S BEST SHORT STORIES

AN ANTHOLOGY
By Some Of Today's Finest Debut Authors

-Edited by Larry Parr

Commonwealth Books Inc., New York

CHAPTER 1

PHILOSOPHY

Ashot Tadevosyan

We use philosophy when we talk or tell about something. That's how we interact with others—through thinking. Were we created in such a manner? Did we evolve that way? Probably not. Life is more complex than thinking and too valuable to rely on thinking only.

When we choose a life partner, we don't think, we feel, as long as the choice isn't spoiled. If we wish to describe Life through thinking—if we dare to do that and are fool enough to try—we need something to serve as an analogy. One possible analogy is fractals. Why? There are many other analogies. All deserve attention, and all are equal. I chose fractals accidentally, the way everything happens in life.

Life fills every second of our being and every millimeter of our space. It includes every object around, even if it is inanimate. If an object was created by man, and we touch it, we can feel life bustling in it. That is the equality of life, to be present in everything created by humans.

We could choose any analogy. All of them bustle. As for being accidental, that property is one of the most-powerful tools that Nature gave us to avoid the dictate of thinking. The accidentality of everyday life assures our freedom. It defends each of us, guarding the uniqueness of every human life. Accidentality is a friend and is one of the supporters of our disobedience in thinking. It brings happy circumstances or good luck.

The word *fractal* describes structures that repeat themselves infinitely. I chose fractals, because they serve as an analogy of our breeding within the infinite. Nature possesses many fractals. They can be found on the Internet. There are mathematical formulas to describe fractals, but to me, fractals are the lines and dots that exist by themselves. They aren't connected to each other but are independent. This independence is another feature of life.

One author said that man comes to life alone and leaves life alone. That means independence, which is like oxygen to human beings. Independence is so native to our hearts that we don't have to prove how essential it is for life. It is one of the ubiquitous one-word definitions of life, assuming life can be defined.

Using a one-word definition enables us to escape the slyness of our thinking. Craftiness and slyness appear when we look at something without the strength of truth or when someone wants to deliberately deceive. Slyness is the road for every human life that leads us to the unknown, thought may be investigated. The road of slyness actually means the road of thinking. Such expeditions are mortally dangerous.

Independence is the essence of human beings. I wish to avoid the question of another animated world. Isn't independence from each other the quality that maintains the border between ourselves and the rest of the animated world?

Fractals nevertheless obey mathematics and thinking. They are the most-analogous structures that resemble Life, because they are infinite in description, but they aren't Life, because they obey thinking. Life obeys nothing and no one. Only a comparison to Life can illustrate how small the infinity of fractals is, how small the infinity of our thinking is, and how small mathematic infinity is, and how small the infinite itself is in the common way people try to define it. Infinite is negligible compared to Life. We can't understand that incompatibility. We can only imagine it.

One of my patients, a young man not yet twenty, had an incurable hereditary disease that destined him to die at a young age. When I met him, he was strong and full of life. His disease hadn't yet affected his appearance.

He was in the hospital for something comparatively simple. He had an easily curable skin infection requiring intravenous antibiotics. With his thick, black hair, someone who met him without knowing about his hereditary disease would be puzzled why he was in the hospital. His girlfriend visited him every day and spent many hours with him. She was as beautiful as a movie star. She was gracious and carried an internal smile that left its mark on her face.

As the man was being treated, I conversed frequently with him about his life. He lived separately from his parents, who didn't support him. He built a small home from grass and tree branches in a public field near the river. Due to his hereditary disease, he no longer worked and lived on social security that paid about $700 a month.

The state also gave him food stamps. His friends helped him out, and he didn't use drugs. He had an intelligent face and might have taken one or two semesters of college. Never depressed, he didn't show any anxiety. He wasn't indifferent to life in common and his own life in particular. It seemed he accepted

his life and destiny. He loved other people, and it showed when he interacted with friends. He enjoyed life, and his tragic fate was far from him at those moments. His girlfriend was in college, where I assumed they met. It seemed important to me that they met accidentally.

He quickly recovered from his infection. There were some difficulties with his outpatient medication, but he said he would solve them. I used the word "tragic" earlier, but it was more applicable to say "idyll" when seeing the couple together. She graciously obeyed him, something that happens to many families around the world.

I don't wish to imply there was something unusual about her that linked her life to his. I saw such things frequently when working in the hospital, and it wouldn't be right to call such situations unnatural or unusual. We saw many couples who were similarly connected, but in the vast majority, it came about from long years spent together, until they functioned as one being.

That wasn't the case with this young man and woman. They were just beginning their life together and hadn't had enough time to cement their souls. Something else kept them together.

Perhaps readers will be upset when I used the word "unusual" when speaking about the young man and woman. That was because I was thinking about them. I didn't see them as a whole. Everyone uses thinking when applying things to the outside world, some more, some less. Women usually use the warmth of their hearts when interacting.

I wondered why the young woman was so attracted to that sick young man. A philosopher, analyzer, scientist, or lay person might have an explanation, and it could be correct. A theologian might say that the sick, poor man knew the pathway to Heaven. The young woman wanted him to take her to Heaven some day, following the road known only to the sick and the poor. A woman would just say that she loved him.

I like that explanation the most. It permits us to avoid the slyness inherent in other explanations and stay away from the craftiness of words. That's how Nature disobeys our thinking. It is too gracious to obey something other than Life. Some people have slyness born in their deepest heart. We may learn from them. The craftiness of their words is righteous, as is the craftiness of us all at times.

Vigor Hugo, the French writer, once said, "There is almost nothing in the world but love." I would dare add that he meant the Earth, the Moon, Jupiter, Saturn, the sun, all other suns, and dust from the stars. Whatever remains after "almost nothing" is the indefinable, or Life.

I never knew what happened to that couple. I discharged him from the hospital after he was cured from his skin infection by the antibiotics. I hoped that all of us wished them a long, happy life. That is the usual way one wishes when we aren't weak. All of us wished he would be cured of his hereditary disease. Our wish may have been so powerful that our thoughts would escape the tenets of thinking, the laws humans impose on nature. Perhaps those wishes would win the battle with his upcoming doom, as some wishes did in the past.

In the remote past, such wishes were called miracles. Miracles can happen when collective wishes for a happy future disobey the laws of thinking, which some call science, which is a weakness of human beings, something temporary. These come in pairs—miracle and science, fate and Life.

Where do our sympathies lie? Sympathies -are another way through which we disobey the things we wrongfully call the laws of nature. These exceptions from common sense, miracles, are the roads by which Life walks into the future.

Many love to talk about miracles. Some people believe in them. Frequently, those believers are women, who know better. We all believe is such things at times, even when we aren't aware of it. That is how we survive the laws we improperly impose on nature in general and the Nature of Man in particular. "Miracle" is the only term by which we can define infinity. Everyone knows that in his own way. We all know the story and are independent.

To clarify why I used suspicious words like disobedience and why I told the story of that young couple, I was talking about disobedience to the rock and the hope for a miracle.

CHAPTER 2

ANTIQUE SHOP

Ashot Tadevosyan

This morning I drove to Bar Harbor on Highway 1A. I left before dawn, calculating my arrival there for sunrise. On the way, I decided to write a new story. Anyone can write a story if he wants too enough. I did. I didn't know what I would write, and I thought about the places I visited in Bar Harbor frequently. One such place was a small antique shop. As I drove, I began composing the story in my mind, planning to finish it at the oceanside.

The antique shop is situated just below the intersection of Albert Meadows and Main Street. I drove past Eden Street and enter the small downtown, turn left, and immediately turn right. The shop was a bit farther down on that narrow street. If I continued down that street, I would come to a small park near the ocean.

The antique shop offered many nice things. I bought a few baubles there in past years, none of them very expensive. The shop occupied two floors of a small, older home. The owner, who lived on the second floor, was a wonderful woman, quick and resourceful, able to offer charming, interesting ancestry for the items she sold. She sometimes checked journals to find analogies to a particular vase or piece of glassware to illustrate her comments. It was always easy to talk with her, as if she'd known me for many years. She was an unobtrusive part of her shop. Like the many items she offered for sale, she stood the test of time.

Another, older woman worked there, too. She retired to Bar Harbor, although she wasn't wealthy. She once told me she paid very low rent compared to other places in town, because she rented the apartment for many years. She even had her own small yard. She was happy and dignified, although her manners were simple. She possessed the natural dignity of a regular person, not like a movie star. She was like crystal-clear water. I loved her, and we spoke whenever I visited the shop.

I tried to learn her dignified manner. She was a good teacher and loved interacting with people. Time made her noble.

The things in the shop imprinted themselves on the two women. They didn't hurry, as if they would live forever, giving customers all the attention they needed. They treated all their clients well.

Once, I saw the owner converse with a man and a woman in English. I overheard some of the phrases and understood they had known each other a long time. They shared common friends and were part of another world I usually didn't interact with, although I felt good hearing them, not alienated.

They spoke about common things anyone in the world would know, and their interaction spread a sense of calm like the calmness that radiated from the items in the shop. The owner could easily handle a more-complicated job than running an antique shop. She once told me she kept her prices fair and didn't try to extract as much profit as possible. When I asked why, she said she loved her job. She hadn't studied antiques intentionally, becoming involved gradually during her life.

The day I wrote this, March 16, the shop was closed, although it would soon open in April or May. I bought several beautiful things there, including some small glasses of Bohemian crystal in different colors. It wasn't a complete set, and they looked as if they had battled through life.

I first took a photo of them and sent it to my wife. She liked the idea, so I bought them. They sit on a kitchen shelf. I use them to drink a little wine when I return home.

Another time, I bought a set of six mugs manufactured in Japan. Each was about 1.5 centimeters in diameter and 2.5 centimeters tall.

They came in a small wooden box, beautifully made, as were many things I collected through my life. Such things become dear to our hearts, as memories of good times or an expression of thoughts we don't reveal, which are part of our essence, wishes, and the inexplicable.

When I drove into Bar Harbor that day, I knew the sun would rise sometime during my arrival. I drove down Eden Street, turned left on Main, and immediately onto Albert Meadows. Within a few feet, I passed the antique shop. Just when I braked to read a small note on the shop door, the sun rose, splashing rays of sunlight on the narrow asphalt road ahead of the car.

I read the note and continued my drive to Grant Park, practically next door to the shop. I stopped in the parking lot and walked to the ocean. It was a cold day, and the water looked cold, too, but I went to the water and put my hands in it. The cool purity of the water was my purpose for the day's drive. I loved doing that.

I thought of writing this story during my drive to town. Tomorrow would be, St. Patrick's Day. I loved that holiday, because, years earlier, I stood for one of my exams connected with my current job. It was an unusual exam, because I had to talk to people who had no connection with my line of work. We were to discuss almost anything but nothing important.

That was similar to the glasses I bought at the shop. Those people had to test how much I loved life. When I used my eyes to ask one of the examiners for help—I couldn't ask directly, because the meeting was being recorded by cameras—he gave me a look that told me everything would be all right, then he nodded slightly.

I asked for help on St. Patrick's Day, and I received it. I wasn't Irish, and I never asked any saint for help. I wasn't even Catholic, but I needed help that day, and even without asking, the saint helped me.

The main thing is to always ask in a way that makes people believe you. Then the saint will help. I had to believe I would receive help when I needed it, even when it was talking during an unimportant examination, something being judged by regular people only.

At the oceanside in Maine, I had thoughts that seemed a bit fantastical. I thought there were probably planets around remote stars, and aliens lived on them. They were older and stronger, their armament more sophisticated. They could move at speeds we could barely imagine, reaching our Earth in seconds. They might think they could conquer Earth, a beautiful, unique planet in the universe. There is no other place so warm and hospitable for life. They even might be jealous of us.

The aliens wouldn't have gods or saints, just sophisticated brains. It came to me that when they attacked, our gods and saints would stand in ranks to defend us, coming from all times and places on Earth. If one of our gods fell, though, the line would be weakened, and our fate would be unknown.

March sixteenth was still winter, a few days before spring. Few shops or cafés remained open during winter in Bar Harbor. Among them was a small shop selling Christmas ornaments. I recently learned that the shop was for sale at a very high price. That surprised me, because the business seemed so profitable.

I learned that the business was established by a couple many years earlier, and they succeeded with it. Success often comes to things that bring joy to others. They couple wanted to leave behind that joy only a few steps from the ocean, one of the many quiet jobs of a beautiful town.

People around the world have their own joy, their small cities and quiet moments. I was happy for them.

My wife and I bought a Christmas decoration there once in the summer. She put it on the bookshelves, where we kept several other small toys. We also had several albums with reproductions of paintings by different artists in different time periods.

One business that remained open during winter was a small café at the beginning of Cottage Street. I often bought breakfast or lunch when I visited the town. From there, I usually went to Sherman's Bookstore to buy paints. Once I bought a sailboat layout. When I was a teen, I dreamed of being a mariner on such a boat. Though I never fulfilled that dream, at least I had it. Dreams are part of quiet human joy.

Thinking of Eden Street reminded me of a meeting there years ago, which I mentioned in another story. I was walking up Main Street to the café, moving away from the intersection with Eden Street. A woman approached with a strange expression and a strange manner of walking. She passed me and continued toward Eden Street, and I wondered if she would be able to reach it.

Standing beside the ocean, I remembered another woman I met years earlier. My friend asked me to pass on a book to her. She was very ill, having been paralyzed in a car accident. The Internet didn't yet exist, and books were highly valued.

I went to her home, and her sister opened the door, guiding me into the room of the paralyzed woman. I opened the door and entered, seeing her in bed with a light-brown headboard. She was covered in an ochre blanket, with her teenage daughter sitting beside her. Thin, blue curtains covered the window. Sunlight passing through them made the woman seem more ill than she was.

Her expression was sad, but when I smiled at her, she returned the smile. I felt pity that such a young woman would be in such condition. She probably felt my thoughts, because her smile became warmer, as did mine. In a second, her eyes sparkled. She felt the sincerity in my smile, and that I understood her pain.

When she livened up, she looked beautiful, and her smile intensified. I saw a healthy, happy woman, though the sincerity of that smile lasted only a second or two.

Then routine settled in, and her face changed to that of a sick, sad woman again.

Wasn't Jesus Christ sincere for longer than that, for eternity? I wondered.

Standing beside the ocean in Maine, I thought, *Shouldn't we learn to have a sincere smile that lasts for eternity? Otherwise,* Homo sapiens *will become* Homo extinct.

I took a breath, bowed to the ocean, and placed my hands in the cold water again. I felt so good near the ocean because of its cold, clear water and fresh air. I knew a lot from reading about the ocean through stories and songs, about the fresh air at the oceanside and its weather, good and bad. I learned many things from stories people told me. Most important was my own knowledge about seas and oceans and the feelings of innumerable people.

I thought about the ocean in French Polynesia and how it was the same as in Japan and Maine. The seashore was different, and their songs and stories were different than the ones I learned in Maine and my childhood. I didn't live in the physical world but in the songs and stories I learned.

The physical world is the servant of songs and stories. I would always be fighting to learn new ones. I didn't want to fight with the seashore of the Polynesians and Japanese, but, if they did, I would. There should be a solution to that, perhaps from business, politics, science, and the routine of daily life.

I thought that the fate of the songs of my childhood and even the ocean before me couldn't be entrusted to a word like *solution*. I would have to rely on the ocean itself.

CHAPTER 3

THE AUDUBON BOOK

Ashot Tadevosyan

Mark Clark lived in a seven-story apartment building on Manhattan's Upper West Side. He lived alone after his wife, Karen, died. Years earlier, the municipality of New York gave them the apartment to rent using funded living, and they lived there for over thirty years.

They had no children. He worked as a gardener in Central Park for forty years, and she was a waitress for her entire life. Their income was enough to pay their rent and allow a little travel and savings. It wasn't much, but it gave them a feeling of security when they retired. Mark still worked occasionally at Central Park.

It was a modest, happy life, and they looked forward to something new at retirement. When younger, they enjoyed attending Broadway shows. They retained that love during their lives, but they couldn't afford to go very often. Still, they felt joy with their lives.

When Karen became ill, Mark cared for her at home, but she was frequently in the hospital. Instead of going to musicals, they took walks in Central Park and in the adjoining streets. Happiness was part of their nature. They were among people who were able to enjoy life in the things most overlooked.

Their marriage moved on without any big disturbances.

There were critical periods in their lives, too. Susan, one of Karen's girlfriends, began paying too much attention to Mark. Karen invited Susan to have dinner with her at a nearby café. At the end of the meal, Karen calmly announced she would beat up Susan if she didn't leave Mark alone.

Susan ended the friendship and later left New York. Mark didn't notice anything except that Susan didn't visit anymore. Karen wasn't the kind who enjoyed fighting. She simply knew Mark was the one with whom she wanted to live until the end. She didn't fight with Susan, but

she warned her what would happen. Karen didn't hate her friend. She understood her, so Karen didn't respond with instinct but with a conversation at a café, because that was the right thing to do.

Mark once had a picnic with his friends at the company. He didn't like how one friend showed affection toward Karen. When the picnic ended, and people were ready to return to their cars, Mark approached the friend and deliberately stepped on his foot, making it look like an accident. The man doubled over with pain, and everyone laughed. The incident was quickly forgotten, but Karen remembered. Karen and Mark never discussed it, but after that, she became more attentive to Mark's wishes.

Karen loved visiting friends occasionally and had many in New York. She brought plenty of news to Mark. His work kept him away from interaction with others for eight hours a day, because he worked outside with plants all day. In addition, there weren't many people in the facility, and all were busy. Mark loved his evenings, when Karen told him stories about people he sometimes didn't know.

Karen was a good storyteller. She didn't add comments, just expressed her emotions. That was the part Mark loved most. The stories weren't that interesting to him, because they were about women.

Once, when Karen said she'd be visiting a friend, and Mark would be alone after work, he decided to stay in Central Park, sitting on a bench near the lake, watching people who ran for fitness. An old gentleman approached. He was reading the notes people left on the benches, and he studied a note on Mark's bench, then he commented on it.

Mark said something, and the man replied, then he became intrusive. Against his will, Mark entered into a conversation, but he wasn't interested and soon left the park.

He returned home, and Karen returned awhile after him. They ate supper, and he told her about the old man he met.

"He's a retired professor," Mark said, "a teacher of philosophy. He said that human beings are the point where the ideal world in the philosophical sense intersects with the physical world."

Karen was combing her hair and didn't hear him clearly. "What did he say?"

Mark repeated his words.

"Was he shaved?"

"What?" Mark was confused.

Karen turned toward him. "Did that man shave in the morning?"

"Why do you ask?"

"Give me an answer, please."

"No, he didn't shave."

"You can't trust the words of a man in a day when he doesn't shave, just like you can't trust the words of a woman who doesn't brush her hair in the morning. Since women always brush or comb their hair each morning, you can trust them."

Mark took offense and thought she was teasing. He left the room and went into the kitchen to make tea. Karen joined him a minute later.

"Please make tea for me, too," she said.

"OK."

Karen hugged him. "You can have a beer with a man who doesn't shave in the morning, but don't keep his words in your mind."

Mark didn't reply.

"Man is a strange creature. The only thing we can be sure of is that Man was given the ability to love. All the rest is just stories, which I bring you from my gossiping girlfriends."

"Are you serious?" Mark laughed.

"Pretty serious. My mother told me that."

That evening, they watched TV and then went to bed.

On the following morning before Mark went to work, he asked, "What if the man had shaved?"

"Then you can pay him money and get a university degree," she replied seriously after some thought.

He retired a year later. Five years after that, Karen became ill. They continued their routine despite her disease and even remained happy. The disease seemed distant when they were together. They enjoyed their friends and relatives.

Then the disease grew out of control. When Karen died, Mark was shocked. He hadn't expected that, because they were so happy right until the end. They knew Karen was dying, but, when it happened, he felt for the first time that life was empty.

During her last months, Karen planned the future for Mark. Her illness didn't overcome her concern for him. She treated Mark as her child, as if that were the only way to use her maternal instincts.

Somehow, Mark survived Karen's death in the fall. He spent most of that winter at home, rarely visiting produce shops. When he went out, he bought enough to last him for a week, so he wouldn't have to go out very often. He avoided their friends.

Finally, he started taking short walks around familiar places. He became attracted to the longer daylight and began to recuperate from his shock. He still experienced bouts of yearning, but that was replaced by sadness and bitterness. His wife and friend was gone, and he had to live alone.

At the end of March, Mark started taking long walks around Central Park. One sunny day in April, he rested on a bench after a one-hour walk and saw a green blush on the tree buds. His mood rose, and he wanted a cup of coffee. Since it was early morning, most places were closed, but he knew a café that should be open.

Mark walked toward the ext and went down the street toward Third Avenue on the East Side. As expected, the café was open. He ordered a coffee and drank it with pleasure. He warmed up after his early walk in the springtime park.

He ordered a croissant with a cup of tea. After drinking the tea, he felt a rare wave of energy and walked toward home. He caught himself thinking he wanted to go home to wake up his wife and suddenly realized she left him forever.

He took short walks while she was alive and even during her illness, but, when she became worse, he started going out an hour earlier so he could get back home before she woke. Once she was awake, he took care of her all day. He did it with love, and she repaid him with thankfulness. They lived together long enough to understand each other without words. Those morning walks during her illness helped him collect his thoughts and feelings. He realized others people's lives were like his. Nobody gave more or less, and joy came from just living.

That spring morning in April, with his bitter sense of loss, he again felt a thirst for life awaken within himself. He was able to comprehend joy again and wanted to find it. It was simple and still accessible.

On his way home, he passed an antique shop. From the corner of his eye, he saw an open Audubon book of birds in the window—an older edition. He stopped to look through the window. He wanted to leaf through the book, so he entered the store, asking to see it.

The seller gave it to him, and Mark sat in a comfortable armchair in the corner, studying the book. It was very expensive, but he wanted to buy it. He returned it to the bookseller and walked into the shop, absentmindedly studying books on the shelves.

Little by little, he became interested. History books were on one set of shelves, children's books on another, and geography books on another, which he caressed with his hand, then the science books he passed with indifference, and art books.

He wished he had a better education. He could have gone to college after high school, but he didn't, because life was too interesting. He went through many jobs in his twenties, never thinking about the future or his career. Changes came in his life unexpectedly. He never planned or fought what happened, and he didn't think very many things were valuable. That wasn't something he was told. That came from within.

He created his own values that he learned from life. Those values were unique for every generation. They might appear to stream from generation to generation, but that was because the packaging seemed the same. The core values had to be reinstalled by each generation. It wasn't a fight that affirmed the values but the sense of worthiness of life, without using words to describe it. It often ran against words. The inner valuation of life and appreciation of everything around came to all people over time.

Some later found they followed that path all their lives, while some suddenly found themselves far from the paths others took.

Then he married Karen, and the company he worked for went bankrupt. They weren't in New York at the time, and he looked for other jobs without success. Happily, Karen earned enough for both of them.

Then Mark started volunteering to work in the town garden twice a week. He was later offered a small, part-time position.

Mark and Karen moved to New York to live with her sister, in Manhattan. Both were lucky enough to find jobs. Karen studied in college for two years after high school and was able to secure a secretarial job at a bank in Manhattan. He became a gardener in Central Park, which was a stroke of luck.

His pension was enough for the rest of his life. Karen lost her job at the bank due to a misunderstanding and started working as a waitress. She stayed with that until she retired. She could have gotten a better job, but she began drinking too much. She chose the deceptive comfort of alcohol instead of the routine of regular life. Though she quit drinking, she wasn't able to return to more-disciplined work.

After she made a full recovery, she found pleasure in a more-relaxed way of living, as if she saw sense in the things around her. That was a rare quality -for men or women. It required a developed mind, watchfulness, and the ability to love life and other people. That last was very rare, though women possessed it more than men. Women were kind from their nature.

Thoughts about the past went through Mark's mind, as he stood before the bookshelves in that small shop. His attention was caught by a red chest with two scratches on it. He assumed it was made at least fifty years earlier, and had been expensive in its day. Perhaps the shop owner inherited it, or maybe it came from his past life and stayed with him.

Old nice things are the threads of love that knit together the past and present, Mark thought.

He didn't have a university degree, but Karen's sister taught him to love reading. When he and Karen lived together, she guided his education. Karen and her sister answered his questions when he didn't understand something he read.

Karen's sister eventually moved to Oregon and remained there. She visited them often during Karen's illness, spending a week or two with them before returning to Oregon. She came to Karen's funeral and told Mark if he suffered too much from his loss, he was welcome to come to Oregon and spend time with her family. Mark, grateful, treated Meggie like his own sister.

Mark slowly walked toward the chest and saw a pile of photographs on it, as if someone placed them there and forgot to collect them. They were old, some with a yellow hue. Mark looked at them. They reminded him of his youth. It seemed they were from the archive of a single family. As he studied them, their faces became familiar, and he noticed how they aged over the years.

His imagination was captured. The photos had belonged to a family over different periods of life. He traced how the children grew up, went to school, then college, had vacations on the sea or on mountains, and celebrated holidays. There were many photos, and Mark spent more than an hour looking through them.

Suddenly, he felt the urge to take them home, so he collected them all and went to the salesperson. "Where'd you get these?" he asked.

"A gentleman who brought in some books gave them to us. He said he didn't need them anymore, but he didn't want to throw them away, either. He said if anyone was interested, the person could have them."

"I'd like to take them home. How much?"

"You don't have to pay anything. They're yours." The salesperson took out a yellow bag and gave it to Mark.

"Thank you." He walked to the exit and went home. He wanted to get back as soon as possible and study the photos again.

At that moment, he thought he acquired a sense of life. The people on the photos would become dear to him. He wanted to frame the photos and place them on the table in the family room. He would call his friends and sit them around the table to tell them the history of that unknown family. Then he would tell his friends what would happen to the grandchildren in the future.

CHAPTER 4

OSCAR THE CLOWN

Oscar Fuentes

The clown didn't hesitate. He ran from the circus really fast. When he looked at the sky, it was blue, the same as the day before. Though it had different clouds, it was still the same blue. His permanent smile could charm any living thing on earth.

He saw her coming out of her yellow door, also wearing a permanent smile. Her smile could tame any furious beast on any circus grounds. Smiling at each other, they walked closer. After a hug and kiss, they smiled and held hands, leaving the performance area for the woods.

Soon, they were under the trees, with rays of light beaming through the leaves. They walked for twenty minutes until they reached the edge of the lake.

She sat on a wooden bench facing the water, and he stood behind her, rubbing her shoulders. Facing the lake, they both smiled at it in silence for a moment.

"What are you thinking, Oscar?" she asked.

"I'm thinking about the unfortunate treatment the animals get at the circus."

"Don't break your head over it, Baby. You know there's nothing we can do."

"It really bothers me, Mariana."

"Not as much as it bothers me."

"You don't know that."

"Yes, I do."

"No, you don't."

"Yes, I do. I notice it each time you do your act."

"Oh?"

"Yeah."

"Get out of town."

"I'm serious," he said. "You know the part where you make the lion walk on his back legs?"

"Yes?"

"And how you make him walk and run around the ring until his tongue hangs all the way out?"

"Yeah? And?"

"You mistreat the animals, too, Mari."

"The lion likes it."

"He doesn't like it."

"He hasn't bitten me."

"Yet."

"That giant cat loves me."

"The fool. You're making him believe he'll get a piece of ass, poor thing. He'll eat you when he finds out you've been messing with his head."

She stood and started back toward the circus without a word, and Oscar followed at a slower pace. Mariana left the woods and headed toward the lion's cage.

Inside his cage, the lion slept like a baby, giving silent roars for snores. He was fifteen feet long, 950 pounds, had a hairy black spot at the tip of his tail, and ten-year-old ruff that went around his head and ears. The front part hung all the way to the floor.

Asleep, he rested carelessly in his cage, breathing loudly, as Mariana walked up to the cage. The cat opened his mind-reading eyes and stared at her. Mariana had an enchanting beauty, as if she were the most-beautiful woman on earth.

"Hello there, my beautiful lion," Mari said. "Why do you always have such a serious expression? No, don't get up. Do you mind if I come in and lie at your side?"

The lion sat on his rear legs and lowered his chest, bringing his majestic head down. She slowly opened the gate and got in, closing the gate behind her. On her knees, she rested against his body.

Twenty-five minutes passed. Out of the woods came Oscar the Clown. He walked toward the lion cage with his permanent smile and saw Mariana sleeping against the lion. The huge cat immediately stood on all fours, knocking Mariana against the bars.

"What the hell's wrong with you?" she shouted.

The lion ignored her and grinned, showing Oscar his long, sharp teeth. Oscar kept walking toward the cage, and the lion sneezed, then gave an earth-shattering roar.

Oscar's heart raced, and he stopped where he was, somewhere between the woods and the cage. His knees shook like an earthquake, and cold sweat ran down his forehead.

Mari stared at Oscar. Her laugh was sinister. She didn't really care for Oscar's feelings.

The lion roared at Oscar again, but Oscar's legs seemed frozen in place. Cold sweat covered his entire body, and he felt a huge knot in his throat. He tried to swallow but failed.

The furious lion didn't like Oscar and felt insecure around him, especially when Mariana was present. The cat knew it was just an animal, unable to transmit human emotion. Oscar had the upper hand, and he knew it. He made love to Mariana many times, but now she was inside the cage.

Another moment passed, then the lion roared again, louder than the first two. Everyone in the circus tents rushed out to see what was wrong. Oscar stood frozen in place.

All the circus freaks surrounded Oscar, including the earless midget, the twelve-foot thin man, the flying acrobats with wings, the six-legged man, the six-year-old Cuban boy with the communist father, the ugliest man on the planet, the manatee man, the talking rabbit, the 450-pound man, the magician, the wolf man, the President of the United States, OJ Simpson, the Colombian mafia, and Medusa, standing beside Oscar with her thirty poisonous snakes for hair.

They stared at the most-beautiful woman on earth and the most-beautiful lion. Mari whispered into the lion's ear, and the freaks became so quiet, they heard wind whistling by. All fifteen individuals standing around Oscar stepped back. Only Oscar remained still, his legs frozen.

Maria calmly unlocked the door to the cage, opened it, and left it that way. The freaks stepped five steps farther away—except Oscar. Mari jumped out, and the lion followed her. She whispered into the lion's ear again.

"Mari," Oscar said, "get him back inside the cage right now!"

"Why don't you tell your monster friends to step back under the tents, eh?"

"All right. You heard her."

They returned to the circus tents and their own business. Mari walked toward Oscar, with the lion right behind. Oscar stepped forward until they were six feet apart. The freaks inside the colorful tents pretended to mind their own business, but they kept shifting their eyes to the drama outside, listening with sharp ears.

Mari and the lion stood side-by-side, with Oscar before them. The lion sat on his hind legs, waiting for Mari to tell him it was OK to eat the man. The fifteen-foot cat was hungry. Oscar heard its stomach growling.

Mari grabbed the lion's cheeks and kissed its mouth. She gave him tongue, as Oscar watched. The lion's eyes opened wider and wider. Mari continued kissing it, and Oscar felt himself becoming jealous, furious, and insulted. He turned red in the face and sweated harder, which dampened his palms.

He was unable to interrupt the kiss, knowing it would mean his painful death. The lion had the upper hand. Maybe it always had, but who knew? The gorgeous Mariana was the only one with the upper hand. Oscar was confused.

The lion breathed heavily, and his heart rate increased. Mariana kept kissing it.

"You'll give him a heart attack, Mari!" Oscar said. "Stop kissing him!"

The lions eyes closed, and his front legs shook. It lost most of its mighty strength. When Mari stopped kissing the lion, there was a pause, then the animals' body tumbled to the ground.

"You killed him!" Oscar said.

"He isn't dead. He's asleep."

"What were you thinking?"

"I was going to feed him a beautiful cloud."

"I'm leaving the circus."

"What?"

"I don't want to be part of it anymore."

"Oh, did I scare you?"

"You aren't funny, Mariana."

"I'm not?"

"You're not as beautiful as I thought, either."

"It was only a stupid joke, Oscar."

"Then I don't understand your sense of humor. I'm leaving."

He stepped back, turned, and walked toward his little trailer, the one with the blue door. Mariana's trailer was right beside it.

WORM IN THE BOTTLE
Oscar Fuentes

Walking into our hotel room, I heard Maria in the shower. The room had a medium-sized kitchen, small dining room, small living room with sofa, a flat-screen TV, a coffee table, and a wooden chair. Two large windows revealed the infinite ocean in a beautiful, breathtaking view. Windsurfers played on the waves. In the distance, a cargo ship slid across the water.

The room had a wooden dresser with wide, tall mirror and a small table with a bottle of Mezcal. Beside the bottle was a small plastic cup with sliced limes, a salt shaker, and two shot glasses. I served myself a shot, put salt on my palm, and squeezed lime into the shot glass. As Maria turned off the shower, I licked salt from my palm and drank the shot.

Maria came out of the bathroom wearing her pink, towel-like robe looking very sexy. The robe was so short it was like a miniskirt. I gave her a *I want you* look, and she gave me a *come and get it* look.

While I started to undress, Maria walked to the small table and served herself a shot, drinking it without salt or lime.

Once I was naked, I got under the sheets, my penis creating a tent under the flowery blanket. Maria released her robe and climbed in beside me.

We fell asleep after sex. When we woke up, it was dark out. Looking out the window, we saw the immense ocean, with the moon rising slowly.

Maria began laughing hysterically. She laughed so much, she released gas, which made me laugh, too. Each time it happened, we looked at each other and laughed even harder. God, we felt so happy.

For the past three months, Maria and I had some horrible arguments. Most were my fault. We annoyed the shit out of each other, and one of us left the house for a few hours. Our arguments were loud and nasty, and I usually broke a mirror, a plate, a coffee mug, or a broomstick—anything breakable.

We were OK, laughing and naked in bed. There were no arguments, no screaming, no hatred, just love and pleasure.

In fifteen minutes, I was dressed and put on cologne. Maria wasn't dressed, and her hair wasn't done. Knowing it would take her about an hour, I decided to go downstairs to the lobby and ask about local bars with live music. Before I left, I went to the little table and raised the Mezcal bottle to pour another shot. I saw a dead yellow worm floating at the bottom of the bottle.

I downed the shot. "I'll be back in a few," I told Maria.

Walking to the lobby, I saw the man at the front desk was the same one who checked us in earlier, though a woman stood beside him with dirty blonde hair and a tight, long, green dress that went to her ankles.

"Mr. Fuentes, how may I help you?"

"Know of a good place to eat, have a few drinks, and listen to live music?"

"Oh, *La Cantina Negra* around the corner is a very nice place," the woman said.

"Yes, Mr. Fuentes," the man said. "That's the place where the beautiful Sofia performs." He pointed at the woman beside him and looked at her with puppy eyes.

"Really?" I asked.

"Yes, Mr. Fuentes," she said. "If you go tonight, I'll dedicate the show to you and your wife."

"That would be very kind of you. I'm sure we'll enjoy it."

She looked deeply into my eyes as if searching for something. I knew she didn't want her companion to know how she looked at me, so I didn't react.

"Well, then, thank you, Sofia. When does the show begin?"

"At ten o'clock," the man said.

"Sounds good. See you both at ten." Leaving them, I returned to my room.

Maria was blow-drying her hair. I sat on the edge of the bed beside the dead worm, took off my shoes, and looked out the window at the full moon. A towel covered Maria's breasts, and her hair hung all the way to her thick, tanned thighs. Half her ass was bare, and I saw her dark, long, sexy legs. She stared at me in the mirror, and I felt very happy.

Maria was almost done drying strips of her hair. I looked at the worm in the bottle, trying to communicate with it in my mind, but there was no reply.

I turned my head and looked at Maria's legs, studying her curves. My gaze returned to her legs, then her beautiful round ass. I felt myself getting excited.

Suddenly, I shouted, "I'll eat you, too, just like the worm!"

Maria jumped. "What the hell was that?" She began laughing.

"Oh, don't mind me. I'm just talking to myself while I wait." I smiled.

I grabbed the bottle and poured Mezcal into the shot glass, then I drank it down. I poured another for myself and one for Maria. I drank mine in one gulp, while she took two.

Maria was finally dressed and perfumed. She dressed to impress and looked good in a tight, glittering, short black dress with black, six-inch heels. I served myself two more shots, and the goddamn worm was still at the bottom of the bottle.

Grabbing the room key, I walked out with Maria behind me, locked the door, and started toward the lobby. We didn't speak on the way to *Cantina Negra*, just walking in silence holding hands.

At the *cantina*, we sat in comfortable brown leather chairs with wooden arms at a round table covered by a white tablecloth. We were only three tables from the stage and one from the middle aisle. A long bar stood near the entrance, and on the stage were a drum set, three microphone stands, a trumpet inside an open case, a pair of conga drums, maracas, and a small man in a pink suit going thought a sound check.

The waiter appeared, and Maria ordered two margaritas. The musicians came out and began tuning loudly. I glanced at my watch, seeing it was already ten o'clock. The small man in the pink suit stood behind the microphone at the center of the stage, adjusted it for his height, and spoke just as the waiter returned with our drinks.

"Good evening, Ladies and Gentlemen! Welcome to *La Cantina Negra*. Tonight we have an excellent show for everyone. Please feel free to get up and dance to the hypnotizing rhythm of our beautiful Sofia!"

The musicians began a mambo. Sofia, emerging from stage left wearing a beautiful feathery dress, walked up to the announcer, kissed his cheek, and waited while he adjusted the mike stand for her before walking off.

She raised her arms up in a V, and all the musicians stopped. Taking the cordless mike, she removed it from the stand and began singing softly without accompaniment. I guess her age at twenty-five. She had long, thick, firm legs, and her voice was similar to Ella Fitzgerald's. I couldn't take my eyes off her. All I wanted was a hot bath with her beside me near a giant window overlooking the ocean, a bottle of Dom Perignon, Esther Phillips playing softly in the background, and a thick sponge to scrub those sexy legs slowly. I had fallen in love, and no one knew it.

Feeling Maria staring at me, I looked at her.

"Close your mouth, will you?" she asked. "You look ridiculous with it hanging open."

I left it open for a moment just to tease her, then I closed it.

Sofia sang a set of ten songs before she took a break. Maria and I finished off three margaritas apiece and were ready for our meal. She signaled the waiter, who came out and took our orders. I caught him eyeing Maria more than once and saw her returning the look, but I didn't say anything. Maria and I were nicely drunk, and an argument would have spoiled things.

The waiter soon brought our food—two chicken quesadillas and two more margaritas. Maria left to use the ladies' room. I noticed the waiter following her down the hall. After pushing my plate aside, I gulped down my margarita.

"Hi, there, Mr. Fuentes," Sofia said, slipping into Maria's chair.

"Sofia! Bravo! You have a beautiful voice. You're very talented." I didn't know what else to say.

"Where's your wife?"

"She went to the washroom."

"Do you have a pen?"

"Yes. Here."

She accepted the pen and wrote down numbers on a paper napkin. "This is my room number." She pointed at one of the numbers. "This is the time I'd like you to come see me. Your wife should be asleep by then."

"Yes, she should, but Sofia, listen...."

"Don't say anything, Mr. Fuentes. I hope you can make it. See you." She stood and walked away.

I watched her go and took a closer look at the napkin before folding it in half and putting it in my pants pocket. She wanted me to meet her at five o'clock in the morning in room thirty-two.

I glanced toward the hall where the washrooms were and saw the waiter walk out drying his face with a napkin and tucking in his shirt. He went behind the bar and served himself a drink. A moment later, Maria walked out, though she looked a bit clumsy.

Sofia and the musicians began their second set. The music was louder. As Maria came closer, I noticed new wrinkles on her dress. It didn't fit her as well as when she left the table. She sat in her chair. Her hair was uncombed, and her lipstick had been rubbed off.

"I feel so relieved, Oscar," she said. "You don't know how relaxed I feel."

"I can imagine." I felt insecure and jealous of the waiter.

"Oh, my God. I forgot about the food. Wow. I feel so drunk, and I don't even realize it."

I reached under the table to touch her long, smooth legs. Through my fingers came memories of all the times I had rediscovered those firm, tanned legs that led me to her melting gold. They were a bit sweaty. I worked my way up her outer thighs to her ass. I didn't feel her panties. She wore them when she left the hotel, but they were gone. Maybe the waiter was wearing them.

Maria devoured her quesadilla, and sweat appeared on her forehead. Without a word, I got up from the table and walked toward the women's restroom. The water was still behind the bar, drying his face and neck. I felt his gaze on me, as I went down the short hall.

When I swung open the door, I startled two young women fixing their hair and makeup in front of a long mirror.

"Don't mind me, Ladies. I'm just looking for my wife's underwear." I knelt on the tile floor to check the three stalls. They were there, just as I thought.

I stood and opened the door of that stall. Picking up the panties, I saw they'd been ripped off her beautiful body. A used condom floated in the toilet.

I took a deep breath, plastered on a smile, and walked out of the stall, while the two women eyed me in the mirror.

One turned and asked, "What are you gonna do to her?"

The other turned and waited for my answer.

"Well? What are you gonna do to her? Are you going to divorce the bitch?"

"Look at him, Rebecca. I think he's going to cry," the other woman said.

"Are you OK, Sir?" Rebecca asked, concerned.

They both wanted to take care of me. A man didn't know what he had until he lost it. I had lost Maria. She was no good.

I always doubted the women who said they loved me. I never really trusted those words. Somehow, I felt they were sleeping with other men even while they were seeing me. For some strange reason, though, I decided to marry Maria. I felt certain and believed in her. I finally felt lucky.

My friends envied me. I enjoyed showing Maria around, because I knew she loved me. She said so. Her friends also said so, but there I was, standing in the ladies' room with Maria's torn panties in my hand. I felt broken and disappointed, barely ten percent human. Glancing at the two young women, I walked out without a word.

Coming out, I looked to my right, where the waiter was still behind the bar. I could tell he'd been waiting for me. He looked curious and seemed ready to fight, but my beef wasn't with him. If I'd been in his shoes, I might've done the same thing. Maria was no ordinary woman. She had perfect proportions and a beautiful face. I couldn't blame the guy.

Ignoring him, I walked toward the table, where Maria was waiting, and Sofia still sang to the loud music. I thought about my food, but the idea made me sick. I sat beside Maria. She finished her quesadilla and ate half of mine.

"Where'd you go?" she asked. "I missed you."

"Come on. Let's get out of here."

"Where are we going?"

"Back to the hotel. I want to show you something."

"I don't want to go to the hotel right now. Let's stay a little longer," she begged.

"No. We need to go now, Maria. Get up."

I signaled the waiter behind the bar, and he sent someone to bring us the bill. I paid in cash, and we left.

"You aren't tipping him?" Maria asked.

I stared into her eyes and started toward the entrance. Maria followed. As we left, I heard the music stop and turned to look for Sofia. The audience stood and applauded, some whistling, but I just kept walking. The waiter was behind the bar, smiling at Maria.

I turned and saw her wave to him with a smile. I swung the door open, and we walked outside. It was only one block to the hotel. Maria followed, but we didn't talk. The stars gleamed overhead. When I slid my hand into my right front pants pocket, I found her torn panties.

It was dark on the streets. The streetlights were out, but I wasn't in darkness. I had finally seen the light. When I tried to swallow, I couldn't.

My throat was knotted. I thought about the bottle of Mezcal in our room and the worm that always stayed at the bottom. He had no worries, no betrayals, nothing. I needed to be inside the bottle.

The first thing Maria did when we got to the room was vomit into the toilet. She drank too much, and all those margaritas and quesadillas came out, ready to be flushed. Righting after vomiting, she stepped into the shower for a moment. When she came out, I handed her a towel and watched her dry her body. Her eyes closed, she walked a few steps to the bed and got under the sheets.

I sat on the edge of the bed, looking at my watch. It was already one o'clock in the morning. I took off my shoes and undressed, then I slid under the sheets with Maria and thought about Sofia.

Maria started to snore. I closed my eyes and tried to sleep, but I knew it was hopeless. I had to meet Sofia at five o'clock.

CHIMNEY SMOKE, GUNPOINT LIZARDS, AND SEXY MAMAS

Oscar Fuentes

In the summer of 2003, I lived in an old, ugly apartment building between Biscayne Boulevard and NE 2nd Avenue off 33rd Street. I had a bitter, mentally unstable landlord who walked around carrying a concealed weapon. I had a part-time gig at History-Miami, the old Historical Museum of Southern Florida, where I gave guided tours of the permanent galleries and wrote historical theater scripts for the Summer Camp program.

Every afternoon during that summer, I arrived home from work and noticed shady people entering and exiting my building, mostly pimps and noticed shady people entering and exiting my building, mostly pimps and prostitutes, the same ones I saw walking the sidewalks while driving down the Boulevard. I also caught a particular barbecue smell circulating in the building's halls.

One day I sat in my writing chair, trying to figure out an ending to three of my stories, when the phone rang.

"Hello?" I asked.

"Oscar?"

"Maybe."

"Hey. This is your landlord."

"What do you want?"

"What do I want? I want my rent, you punk!"

I hung up. I hated people who cursed on the phone, especially annoying landlords. He was the worst I ever had. I was only two days late after the first of the month, and he was already calling the cops on me.

I heard a knock on the door. I had a bad feeling about it, but I answered and saw my neighbor, the seventy-five-year-old stripper. She carried a six pack of Heineken, so I let her in. She always wore a miniskirt, and the loose skin on her legs hung down. She had yellow, twisted teeth and always bragged about how, in her youth, she was the hottest stripper in Miami. Now she was old, sick, and very tired.

We drank the beer and discussed the poetry of life. I mentioned the BBQ smell in the building. She looked at me with frozen eyes and slowly pointed out my back window.

"Oscar, there's a smoky chimney out there."

I walked over to look and sure enough, a smoky chimney was right outside my window. I didn't ask about it, assuming I'd go down and see for myself.

After a while, she left, and I returned to my writing. The phone rang again.

"Yeah?"

"Goddamn it, Oscar, I swear, you hang up on me one more time, and I'll put a bomb on your doorknob."

"What do you want? My rent?"

"*My* rent. It's mine!"

"Come pick it up."

"When?"

"Right now, you lizard."

"Oscar, if I go there and don't find you, I swear to God...."

I hung up again. I hated people bitching on my phone.

Someone knocked three times on the door. I opened it and saw a giant lizard wearing funky sunglasses, shorts, sandals, and a funny haircut. It also resembled an iguana, but it was the landlord.

"What are you doing here?" I demanded.

"Oscar, I've had it up to here with you." He pointed at his stomach.

He was a tall, heavyset man of 300 pounds who always smoked cigars. He chewed breath mints, giving him tobacco minty breath. As usual, he looked insane and dangerous.

"Your rent is five days late!" He drew his .45 and pointed it at my left knee.

I froze.

He walked around me into the apartment and aimed at my back. "I want my money. Where is it?"

"Look, Pops, just take it easy."

"I've been taking it easy too long."

"Look, Man, I don't have the money here in the apartment."

"What?"

"We gotta drive to the bank on Coral Way. My car's out of gas."

"No problem. We'll use mine."

He drove, steering with his left hand while keeping the .45 aimed at my stomach with his right. I didn't have to give him directions. He knew all the shortcuts. He was also a speed-driving lizard, like those I saw on the road who were always enraged, looking for someone to hit with his bumper.

He hit an old lady crossing the street. She looked like the stripper from my building, but it wasn't her. When I looked again, she was already on her feet and walking away as if nothing happened.

We finally reached the bank, only to find it closed. Most closed at 5:00, but this one closed at 4:45. The lizard made me knock on the glass, but the employees didn't bother looking, as they counted out their tills for the day.

I was glad the bank was closed, though, because my account was empty. Seeing my chance, I kicked the gun from his hand, grabbed it, and aimed at him. I smelled shit running down his pants.

"This is where you lose, Lizard," I said.

"You got a bomb on your doorknob, Oscar."

"That's why you'll open it for me."

"In your wildest dreams!" He ran off with surprising speed.

He was a coward, a yellow lizard, one of the sorry-ass lizards I saw in people's yards.

I looked at my watch and saw it was 5:15, and I remembered I had a date with a hot mama, the hottest ever. I walked back to the car and saw the lizard left the keys in it, so I drove off down the congested streets.

Back at the apartment, I stood outside the door, thinking. There was a 50% chance I had a bomb attached to the doorknob, so I broke in through the kitchen window. I saw a black plastic device with a blinking light on the doorknob that resembled a toy.

When I walked closer, I saw it was just a toy after all. I laughed and knew the lizard had finally lost his mind, because the thing had an on/off switch. I turned it off and dropped it to the wood floor.

After a quick shower, I dressed and heard the engine of my date's car pulling into the parking area. Without thinking there could have been a real bomb on my door, I opened it, walked out, and closed it, locking it behind me.

I opened my date's passenger door and got in. Just changing radio stations, she looked up at me.

"Where to?" she asked.

"The City Port."

"Why?"

"Sweetness, I don't really care where we go. Anywhere you want is fine."

She smiled, showing beautiful teeth. Then she stopped and pointed at the building beside mine. "What's that smoky chimney?"

We drove around the block on NE 2nd Avenue and finally saw the front of the building with the chimney. It was Van Orsdel's Crematorium. I sat in the car in shock. It all made morbid sense—the dust on my windowsill wasn't dust, and the BBQ smell in the halls had nothing to do with BBQ.

THE DEVIL WHO FEEDS MY EGO
Oscar Fuentes

I worked at the bar for thirteen hours, serving drinks, when the phone rang.

"Hello?" I asked.

"Is this Oscar?"

"Perhaps."

"What do you mean, perhaps? Are you or aren't you?"

"All right. You've got me. What's the deal, and who the hell is this?"

"This is Satan."

"What?"

"That's right. Satan, the Devil, Lucifer, whatever works for you."

"How may I help you?"

"The question is, how can you help yourself?"

"Oh, I see. OK, then. Suck ass, Satan." I hung up, took a small kitchen knife from under the bar, and began cutting the phone cord. It took a while, but I finally did it.

I realized he could have just disconnected it. *Was that really the devil?*

A guy with a glass eye came over to the bar and said, "A scotch with water, please."

I poured him a strong one, because I didn't want him coming back soon with that eye, scaring away my tips.

"Look, Buddy," I said, "I just gave you ten straight lines of scotch so you can sit quietly in that corner and take small sips, taking your time with the drink, OK?"

"Huh?"

"You scare people with that glass eyeball of yours, Baby. Seriously, you do."

"What? Are you scratching my balls?"

"Look, Brother. Let me put it to you this way. I need to make some good tips tonight. If you hang around with that horrible eye of yours, you'll scare off my customers."

He scratched his elbows, then his left knee, then his nose, belly, and butt. It was clear he was a nut case. He winked his good eye at me, while the other reflected horror. When he finally walked away, he was clumsy as hell.

As soon as he was in his corner, the phone rang again. I stared, as it rang three times, though it was disconnected. I didn't answer. After a while, it stopped, and I poured myself a scotch with a splash of water, downing it in one gulp.

The phone rang again, and I answered. "Yeah?"

"Your time's running out, Oscar! Out! Out!"

"Satan, is this you again?"

"Yeah."

"Good. I'm glad you called. Why don't you stop by for a drink with me?"

"I'll be there in a minute."

I hung the receiver back in its cradle and stared at the cut cord, where small electrical sparks popped from the cut end.

Everything started shaking—the walls, floor, ceiling, bar, and bottles. Some bottles feel to the floor, but none broke.

An earthquake in Miami? I wondered.

Then it hit me. He really was the devil, and he was coming over. Who else could it be?

The shaking stopped, and my heart beat faster. I looked around without seeing anyone who looked like the devil, but what did he really look like?"

I searched again and saw the guy with the glass eye in the corner, sipping scotch. My heart pounded, and sweat beaded on my forehead and dropped down the sides of my face.

Everything shook again, the bottles, walls, and ceiling, then Satan suddenly stood before me on the other side of the counter, looking ready to order a drink.

"Satan?" I asked.

"Yes," he said softly.

"Can you stop the shaking?"

It stopped. He smiled and said, "I love making an entrance."

"Why 666?"

"Because 665 other demons auditioned, but none made the cut." He sounded like he answered that one a million times.

He wasn't bad looking, either. Some would call him beautiful.

"Why not go into show biz?" I asked. "You've got the looks."

"Been there, done that. I hated it, and I hate talking about it."

"Let me pour you a strong one."

"Yeah," he replied. "Why not ten lines from each of the bottles?"

"You got it." He gave him exactly what he asked for. When I handed him the drink, he drank it in one gulp, then he looked depressed.

"Give me two more of those."

I made the drinks and handed them to him. He slammed them down in rapid succession.

"Why me?" I asked.

"Why you what?"

"Why'd you come looking for me?"

"Oh, well, you're the only one around here who doesn't fear me."

I was quiet for a moment, and then I poured a scotch and downed it in one hit. I almost choked on it, and my eyes felt watery and heavy, then I felt brave again. I'd never felt so brave before. I was invincible. I was ready to kick Satan's ass on the spot, but first, I wanted to make sure why he feared me.

"What makes you fear me?" I asked.

"I fear your genius."

"Fair enough." The angel from hell knew how to feed my ego. Still, my genius alone wasn't enough reason for his fear. I had the feeling he didn't want to tell me the real reason.

"You know what, Satan?"

"What?"

"I'm not convinced you fear my genius. I think there's something you aren't telling me."

"You're too much. You're right. There's something I'm not telling you."

"What is it?"

"I've been following your life story since you were born. Since the day of your birth, you've been the brightest of them all. Now, at the age of thirty-five, without even knowing it, you've written masterpieces that will someday make you immortal."

"Why are you being so nice to me? Aren't you supposed to be all mean and evil? I don't know, Satan. I get the feeling you're scratching my balls."

He became pensive, rolling his bloodshot eyes right and left. "All right. You got me again. I'll tell you the reason I came here. First, I wanted a couple of You got me again. I'll tell you the reason I came here. First, I wanted a couple of free drinks. Second, you're fearless. You don't fear anything, even me."

"True." *Damn*, I thought, *he makes me feel like a million dollars.*

"Oscar, I need your help."

"What is it?"

"About two days ago, a woman asked me for a favor. She wanted immortality and lots of money. I told her what she wanted came with a price. She told me she'd do anything I wanted. I told her I wanted her to go on six dates with me for six nights. Each night, I'd make love to her six times until sunrise."

"Is she a looker?"

"She's a knockout, and she didn't have any problem with those conditions."

"So what do you need from me?"

"Well, I need you to take over my duties for me."

"Duties? What kind of duties?"

"For the next six nights, I'll be showing her the amusement park I have down in hell."

"Amusement park?"

"That's right. A few of those nights, I'll take her to this little love shack I created in the core of the moon."

"Inside the moon?"

"That's right, Baby. I want you to cover my duties here on earth."

"That's it?"

"That's it."

"Are you sure?"

"Why would I lie to you?"

"Because you're Satan."

"Good answer, but you're safe, Oscar. No need to worry." He smiled.

"What's in it for me?"

"Whatever you want."

"How do I know you'll keep your word?" I asked.

"Stop being a bitch about it and just do it. You'll get your reward."

I didn't respond. For some reason, I trusted him. He fed my ego enough for me to like him. I felt extremely flattered that he asked me for a favor.

We stood across the bar from each other without speaking. I poured him another round of scotch. He drank half, placed the glass on the bar, and pointed at it with a finger. I looked at the shot glass, then at him. With his eyes, he offered me the second half of the scotch.

I drank it, then I took out a pack of Camels and lit one.

"You're a badass, Oscar," he said with a spark in his mind-reading eyes.

"I know."

"So what'll it be, Biscayne Poet?"

"Six nights?"

"Yeah. Six nights."

"All right. I'll do it."

"You're a good sport, Oscar. Don't worry. I'll hook you up." He disappeared.

I felt a knot in my throat. My ego was still pumped. I poured another scotch and saw the guy with the glass eye get up from his corner and walk even clumsier than before. He went right past me and out the door.

I downed the scotch in one gulp without feeling it. My ego was still pumped, and I was still braver than ever. I couldn't believe Satan came all the way from hell to ask me for a favor just so he could get a piece of human ass. That bastard sure knew how to feed my ego.

CONTAMINATED BY ROMANCE

Oscar Fuentes

It was Salsa night in Washington, DC. The trombone spoke my language, and my feet listened happily. Earlier I took the Metro to DuPont Circle to meet her at 10:30 PM at ESL, the Eighteenth Street Lounge. The neon lights at the bar made her eyes a brighter blue.

She ordered a Maker's Mark, and, as I held a beer in one hand, Salsa music moved my legs. In the loud music, our eyes exchanged telepathic messages. Disco lights flashed through the room and onto her blue eyes. Dancing, we laughed. When we spun, our eyes locked again, and, in the shadows of the flash, the strangest, most-beautiful feelings came to me. I felt vulnerable and alive. The music was so loud, we could speak only with our eyes, and with each spin, we said different things.

I wish I didn't have to go back to Miami.
Yeah. I wish you could stay longer.
I feel so happy right now.
Me, too.
You dance so well.
So do you.
I want to kiss you.
I hope he kisses me.
No. She'd totally reject a kiss.
We kept dancing.

Though the last Metro of the night passed, still we danced. My hands on her waist, I gave her another spin. There was a good chance I'd never see her again.

Another spin, and we pulled our bodies together to the beat of the Latin bass line. Time passed quickly. I felt incredibly lucky. It happened so fast.

I snapped out of it when I saw her come close to kiss me on the sidewalk.

"It was so nice meeting you," she said. "Love, Muah." She pulled away quickly and waved to a cab.

Speechless, I raised my hand to wave. "Yes. Nice meeting you, too. Thanks for inviting me out to Salsa!"

She was already inside her cab, so I waved for one of my own.

"Where to?" the cabbie asked.

"Brookland, please."

"That's too far for me. Sorry."

"You OK, Oscar?" she called.

"Yes! No worries!" I waved another one down and got in. "Brookland Station, please."

The tail lights of her cab disappeared into the cold DC night. *Farewell to the Girl with the Sun in Her Eyes* played in my mind. I felt sad and happy. I was alone again, with the fresh memory of her eyes, the music, and the flashing lights.

How could time pass so quickly?

Her name was on the tip of my tongue. I knew I experienced a powerful poem on my only night out with Felicia in Washington, DC.

I was back in Miami the following day, on Biscayne Boulevard. My Dodge Dart drove itself to the Bay to welcome me back. The Vagabond Hotel was just days away. The sunset colors on the bay were electric orange and purple.

With my eyes closed, I felt the Biscayne wind remind me I was home. I got into the Dart and drove north on the boulevard past Thirty-Sixth Street. Through the rearview mirror, neon motel lights flickered.

I stopped on red, drove again on green. My mind was on my journey to DC. That was when she texted.

Hi, Biscayne Poet! Hope you had a nice flight!

My heart skipped a beat, and I texted back.

Hi. Yes, it was a nice flight. Thanks for the Salsa dancing. That was a lot of fun.

Time went by too fast, though. I wish we could have talked more.

I know. I was going to suggest an early breakfast, but I knew you were heading back to Miami early, and it was already super late.

LOL. Yeah. Guess I need to come back to DC for more Salsa and you.

We texted back and forth for three weeks. Texting evolved into long phone calls, then Skype calls. We developed a routine, with good-morning voice messages and late-night phone talks with heavy breathing.

One day, I texted, *I'm gonna buy a plane ticket so I can see you again.*

I wish! I can't go to Miami right now. I'm way too busy here with dance, work, and all, but can you come to m

Actually, I believe I can. I began searching online for a plane ticket.

I booked a flight for June 25, and it was only May 10. Thank God I bought that ticket. I knew there was a good chance I'd die of lustful desperation if I didn't make some effort to see her again.

She was ecstatic when I told her on a phone call. "Oh, my God! Thank you for doing that! That's like forty-five days away! I don't think I can wait that long!" She laughed excitedly.

I imagined my Jet Blue Airlines flight taking off back to DC and dropping me onto her bed.

Long days that felt like weeks dissolved into texts and imaginative projections of how we would love each other come June 25, but it was only May 12. The Vagabond was just one day away.

Suddenly, she called and said, "Babe, guess what?"

"What?"

"I'm coming to Miami on June sixth!"

"What? How? No way! This is great!"

"I can't wait until June twenty-fifth, so I'm coming to you."

I thought of staying alone at the Vagabond Hotel, writing a few feet from Biscayne Boulevard, with its picture-perfect days and pretty women in fashionable smiles. There were many opportunities to fool around for an artist. Interestingly enough, for the first time in a long while and despite the distance between Washington and Miami, I was happy to be in a long-distance phone affair with my sweet Felicia.

It was May 14, 2015, my first night at the Vagabond to kick off my five-day writer's residency. My musicians and I gave a stellar performance by the pool and felt great afterward. We sounded phenomenal. Matt's saxophone seemed on fire. Carl's guitar was smoking. Just like the old days, the poetry jazz combo was back for one n4ight only, just a few feet from the Boulevard. My Dodge Dart was parked beside the hotel, and my friends and I sat at the bar across the pool with its four streams splashing down.

On May 15, I felt I really appreciated the hotel. It felt beachy, antique and stylish, *vagabundeando* with style. It was nice to know there was a place for hybrid vagabonds like us. Life was a long train that came and went. Felicia was on my mind. The mid-century architecture inspired my muse, but Felicia was there again. That hopeful feeling pushed us off a cliff, parachuting into the vagabond spirit, while a mid-century state of mind poured its heart out.

At 12:41 PM, I left the hotel for my Dart. The Coppertone girl with her pooch across Biscayne Boulevard made me stop. I sighed, thinking, *This is home.*

Getting on the Boulevard, I drove south. Through the rearview mirror, I saw the string of motels behind me. The Biscayne wind in my lungs slowly turned me into a wolf ready to howl. I stopped at red, drove on green. I thought again of my time in DC and that dance floor, remembering Salsa moves I improvised flawlessly, spinning her until her blue eyes flashed in the dark, while the club's winking lights made her appear and disappear.

It happened too fast. She was visiting me on June 6, and I would visit her on June 25. Somehow, it made perfect sense.

Turning left on Thirty-Fifth Street, I headed down to the Bay for my daily Miami ritual to honor the story of the poet who fell in love with the shadow of death, the raven-haired beauty who lived under the waters of Biscayne Bay. Her lover was last seen walking alone with her, not fearing the danger.

"Now the sun from tower to tower," he told her, flirting and laughing with Lady Death. "The hammers. The hammers. Because yesterday in my verse, I heard the clapping of your bony palms, and you gave ice to my voice and an edge to my tragic life. I'll sing for you the flesh you don't have, your missing eyes, the red lips that used to receive kisses. Today and from here on, my sweetness, death of mine. Oh, how good to be alone with you and these blowing winds of my Biscayne."

I stared out at the Bay, sighing and smiling at the thought. Finally, I got back in the Dart and drove south to Twentieth Street. Right before making the right turn on Twentieth, I realized I wasn't alone in the car. She sat beside me, caressing my shoulders as I drove, heading over to Kush for some gator bites and a beer.

The muse didn't just live under the waters of Biscayne Bay. She also lived in the Wynwood wind, in the breeze streaming through my Dart, with immortality that never felt more real. Perhaps it was a call to action. *Bah*, replied the lazy wolf in my blood. I needed to return to the Vagabond and continue writing.

I reached Kush on the corner building of North Miami and Twentieth Street, the same building where Cornerstone used to be. Inside, the wall painting of Purvis Young looked through me, so I turned to face the North Miami Avenue window instead. I sipped my beer, waiting for my gator bites.

Felicia texted me a video of her tango performance in front of the Washington Monument. She looked beautiful in her red dress with a red flower behind her left ear. I couldn't wait to see her.

June 6 would arrive soon enough. My Vagabond retreat will have passed by then. The Vagabond Hotel book project was already underway, another Miami river of ink contaminated by romance.

CHAPTER 5

THE ROCK

Ashot Tadevosyan

I have lived in the United States for twenty years. I love this country and its people, my colleagues and neighbors. I loved my neighbors when I left Armenia and relocated here.

Andrew was one of my Armenian neighbors. That isn't an Armenian name, but he was a pure Armenian with ancestry back to the foothills of Mount Ararat, the same Mount where Noah's Ark moored after the Flood.

The country of Armenia surrounds Mount Ararat. It is clearly visible from every place in Yerevan, the capitol. It shone in the distance when I once played chess with Andrew on my apartment balcony.

He was a strong player who had studied chess. By profession, he was a mathematician, teaching geometry at one of the universities in Yerevan. Though he died while I was still living in Armenia, his story isn't a sad one.

We played chess in nice weather on the balcony, drinking coffee prepared by my wife, when Andrew suddenly asked, "Would you prefer to leave your children an inheritance of one million dollars, or would you like God to protect them their entire lives?"

"I don't know," I replied.

We continued playing. He usually won. Once he told me I was the best chess player among our neighbors except him. Our building had fourteen floors, with four apartments on each. It sat in a newer part of the city. It was a time of war and blockade in Armenia. The winters were very cold due to lack of fuel and electricity. During the summers, when the temperature was above thirty-five-degrees Celsius, there was often no running water in our building. That happened to all the buildings in Yerevan and the other towns throughout Armenia. Such things happened to many countries throughout history, but only when it happens to someone can he realize just what it feels like. I still recall that feeling and was lucky enough to survive the situation. Andrew, who was older, didn't.

It was close to New Year's Day, a big holiday in Armenia. In Soviet times, people didn't usually celebrate Christ's Birthday on that particular day, so the joy of life splashed out on New Year's Day. It wasn't forbidden, but it fell out of custom. The state slowly squeezed all the humanness from the people during the preceding seventy years. Despite the pressure from the state, people revolted and built a beautiful country. The state broke down by revolutionaries, not the West as claimed in many newspapers.

It was late autumn, and I returned home from work. I spent several hours in the city, and it was almost eleven o'clock that night. It was already cold. We had an unusually cold autumn and winter in Yerevan.

I parked my car and entered the building. As usual, the elevator didn't work due to lack of electricity, so I started climbing the stairs to my apartment on the fourteenth floor. It wasn't a penthouse. That word didn't apply to buildings in Armenia at that time. People who lived on the top floor felt punished for it.

On one to the entryways to the staircase, I met a neighbor. We talked about the weather and other things.

"Have you heard the news?" he asked in a gloating voice.

"What news?" I asked.

"Andrew is building a garage for A."

A was a good man, a teacher at one of the universities in the city. For some people, serving another was a shameful thing. My neighbor felt that way.

"Listen," the neighbor said. "Do you hear the hammer?"

I strained my ears and heard muffled hammering. "What is that?"

"Andrew's breaking the rock in the garage."

"What do you mean?"

"A was building the garage and came across the rock. They didn't have anything to remove it, or it was too expensive. I don't know why they quit. He hired Andrew to break it. Andrew is physically fit, but he has to work with a hammer and chisel. He needs the money for New Year. Everyone wants to have a holiday dinner table."

That was during the time when the Soviet Union broke down, and everything was in turmoil. Salaries were low, and all goods had high prices.

Saying nothing to my neighbor, I resumed my climb.

I played chess with Andrew the following weekend.

"I've almost finished with the rock," he told me proudly. "Only I could break such a rock. I did a job like this once when I was a student at university and needed the money. It's the only way I can provide for my family."

A week or two passed. I returned home just before New Year's Day, once again late at night. It was cold, with a strong wind, though there was no snow. The absence of snow made the weather and wind seem especially cold. I had very little gas in my car. It had been difficult finding gas for the past few days, and it was very expensive when it was available. People sometimes bought only two or three liters to allow very short trips.

I wondered if I had enough to reach home. There was still no electricity, no water, and scant bread. My car stopped running. I tried to get gas from other cars that were running, and two stopped to help, but neither of them could drain any fuel from their tanks, because they were almost empty, too.

The night grew darker, and cars became scarce. Finally, another car stopped, and the driver asked, "What happened?"

"I ran out of fuel."

He thought for a moment. "I can help, but I'm in a difficult situation. I bought a canister of gas today. It was very expensive, more the twice the usual price."

I knew that high demand made the usual price terribly high, but with the holiday and our borders being almost closed, it was even more expensive than usual.

"I was planned an important business trip tomorrow," he said, "but I've changed my mind. I'd better spend the money for our holiday dinner table. I can give you the gas, but only the whole canister at the same price I paid."

He paused to curse the middlemen who raised gas prices right before the holidays.

I had little choice and thanked him. I felt certain he was being honest with me. He helped me put the gas into my tank. We spoke a little, and we both cursed the middlemen again.

After we parted, I drove home. We had a nice holiday. Holidays are always festive in Armenia. We visited Andrew, and he and his wife visited us. We drank a little homemade Armenian alcohol, made from cornel tree fruit that grew in the mountains.

I rarely drank alcohol, but Andrew said it was prepared in the small village where he was born. I agreed to try it. We had a good time afterward, playing chess. As usual, he won.

CHAPTER 6

THE GRAND STAND

Margreta Klassen

The crowd cheered, as the team ran onto the field, their white helmets gleaming under the glare of the lights. Matt Benson, stuffing his hands into his gray overcoat pockets, watched his breath spout misty jets against the cold night air. This was it—the big game.

The trouble was, it wasn't really the first big game. There were so many, and each time they ended, he was a little older and not much wiser. He glanced idly at the stands, which were almost full. Seeing his wife huddled over the statistics sheet, he grasped the brim of his tattered hat in their secret signal. She said that hat was his good-luck charm. Their little ritual was that he saluted her by touching it.

Out in the field, Matt's boys were warming up. The slap of hands interspersed with the hustle talk had a rhythmic beat that still made his blood surge. Fairfield was out for the district championship. There were only 2,500 people in Fairfield, but most were up in the bleachers, their eyes glistening before the prospective battle.

Not that small towns have a corner on the game, Matt thought, remembering how excited he and Jane were when he was offered the chance to coach under Sid Johnson at the university up state. His lips twitched at the memory.

Couple of crazy kids, he thought.

They bought the hat that night. It was crisp and jaunty then, almost a mountain-climber's hat. He certainly had plenty of mountains to climb.

"Stand up for the kickoff! Everybody up!"

Matt stopped pacing and braced himself. Fairfield's quarterback wrapped his fingers around the ball and pulled it to him. The game was underway.

Matt crouched on the sidelines. The lights blurred, as he stared at the two teams, until they became any and all teams, all of his teams, blurring and sliding together until they formed a collage of helmets with dark, smeary eyes in scared white faces, ready to duel, while the crowd shouted lustily, "Kill! Kill! Kill!"

He shook his head and closed his eyes to stop the vision. Had it really been fourteen years since he came to the university? What happened? What was he doing there? There was another small town once before. Janie liked it. That was state, after he finished with Johnson. He won every game that first year, and they had dinner invitations, friendly people, a big write-up in the papers, and a new car. That was style. His son was born there.

It was a familiar town. The men made jokes and laughed when Mark was born.

"'Nother star, huh, Matt? Yes, sirree, look at those shoulders."

Yeah, look at 'em, he thought, then he lunged to his feet and shook his fist at his linemen.

"Keep 'em down! Keep 'em down!"

"Stand up for the kickoff! Stand up!"

What do they mean, kick? He was confused. Center City was ahead. He paced nervously, scuffing the chalk lines and clenching his fists in his pockets. Those green-white kids out there had to win. Didn't they know it meant his job? Where would a guy find another coaching job at fifty-five? Didn't they know that? Sweat trickled down the back of his neck and slid icily under his shirt collar.

"Let's go, Big Team, let's go!" people chanted.

Matt pleaded with his eyes, then stared at the ground. When he had to plead, something was wrong. He remembered the day when Mark ran into the house, tears on his face. Matt had winning years, then he began losing. His confused son threw himself against Matt's legs.

"Dad? The kids say you got fired, and we gotta move. They're crazy, aren't they? Dad?" *How could I answer that?* he wondered. *How could I say, "I tried, Mark?" How could I answer the look in Janie's eyes or the fear in my own gut?*

He took a smaller job in a smaller town, with smaller people telling him how and when to "win, baby, win." There was no time for losers, no cheers for bum scores, but there was plenty of fear burning and nagging, sinking and rising in great, oozing gobs that haunted him.

"Hey, hey! Take it away!" the crowd shouted.

Matt watched desperately. *God, they're trying, aren't they?* Trying didn't always get it, though, did it?

The clock lights blinked down to zero. The game was over. Matt stood there feeling numbness slither over him. He patted the boys awkwardly, as they stumbled off the field.

It was only a game, wasn't it? Wasn't it?

All hail.

LOCAL CELEBRITY

Margreta Klassen

The local radio station interrupted its pulsing, primitive beat with a bleating news announcement.

"Local boy reported lost on mountain exploration. KMFK is first with breaking news whenever and wherever it happens. Details on the 5:55 news broadcast. Remember, Listeners—text or phone in wherever you are and win cash for on-the-spot news reporting!"

If Dave Blake had heard that, he might have laughed. He thought it would be exciting to be the first with the worst, but he was in no position to cash in on the opportunity.

Twilight fingered the mountaintops. Rose-gold, the tallest peak reflected the dying sun, as it kissed the snow-clad summit. It was cold all day, but climbing was exhilarating in the brisk air. At the lower levels, the long-needled pines exhaled their pungent scent, making Dave's long legs stride faster across their crispness. Patches of icy snow nestled against the north sides of the trees. Occasionally, a saucy squirrel scrambled up a limb and chattered disdain upon the stumbling intruder in the wilderness.

I should have started back earlier, he realized, as black shadows slid down the rocky ravines.

There's an urgency that keeps you going upward, he thought, *something that pulls and whispers and sings. Suddenly, you look back and wonder where you came from. Below, everything is a green, gold, and gray mass. It's indistinguishable, but I passed through there.*

He wondered how long he left his mark down below. It might last until the night wind shifted the fallen leaves or the snow drifted again. Maybe it was already gone.

At 5:58, the radio announcer interviewed an officer at the sheriff's station. "Officer, can you tell us the latest word on the boy reported lost in the mountains?"

The radio beeped, indicating a live news contact.

"Well, at this time, there isn't much to report. Rescue units will be ready for daylight, but, well, it's getting dark now. Not much we can do at night."

"I see. Thank you very much, Officer. There you have it, KMFK listeners, another on-the-spot news report brought to you by your on-the-spot news station."

Dave heard it and shrugged, as blackness bloomed on the ledge where he stood. He hadn't reached the top despite his youthful vigor and the mountain's song. Where he gazed a few minutes earlier, seeing breath-taking color, had turned nondescript. He zipped his red nylon parka tighter and rubbed his hands until they tingled. He carried a small canteen of water, and he ate late in the afternoon. Touching his index finger to the tip of his nose, he felt the newly rubbed warmth alien to the sharp, cold ridge. He wondered if his family would be concerned. He was past the age of checking in, but he told a friend he wanted to try for the top.

You might say I'm lost, he thought, *because I don't know if I should go up or down. Yet I'm here, and it feels as if the world is lost.*

He knew it would get colder, as night settled into the cradle of the ravines and ledges. He was also experienced enough to know that traveling much farther in the icy stillness would be of little value, because the blackness would interfere with his sense of gravity. His feet felt the rocks, and his hands touched the loose sides of the mountain, but his sense of direction wouldn't return until dawn.

He went forward cautiously. *It's reassuring,* he told himself, *that a man can tell by his own anatomy what's forward or back, but north or south, up or down, lost or found...? How can you find that on the side of a giant, dark, shifting mountain?*

He put his hands out to the right, and a shower of smooth, round, granite pebbles rolled past, echoing in the first stillness of the night.

"Damn!"

The expletive hung in the air, suspended by the cold. He had to find shelter. The temperature could easily drop to 12° at that time of year. While his tight jeans and heavy boots and parka provided a sense of lightness and freedom on the ascent, the temperature crept through any crevice in his clothing, so he was getting uncomfortable.

There was no trail on that side of the mountain, which was why he chose it. It was his defiant gesture at those who scorned his generation as lazy and spiritless.

He dropped to his knees, feeling the ground with his fingertips. One foot at a time, he crept along the mountain, his right side pressing against the rocky surface. Part of him wondered what time it was.

Stopping, he hunched into a crouch and unbuckled his canteen. The water felt lukewarm in contrast with the frosty air. He wished for hot coffee laced with sugar, and his stomach growled in protest. The noise comforted him in the silence. As he replaced the canteen, his stiff fingers touched the cold buckle. He struggled with it, and the container's awkward shape burst from his hands like a bullet from a gun. As he listened, he heard it ricochet down the mountain.

Now I've done it. No food, water, or smart phone. Not even matches or a flashlight. Should I keep moving?

Of course, you idiot, his thoughts replied.

I don't know where I'm going

You'll freeze if you stay here.

I might fall.

You'll freeze there, too.

He visualized a fireplace, smelled food cooking in the kitchen, and heard his mother laugh. He was afraid. Where had the mountain's song gone? Who said you could never go home?

He inhaled, and the cold air hit his nostrils and chilled his throat, while his lungs fought to warm it. He crawled a foot, then another. More rocks fell.

He cried out. Moving his left hand forward, he reached to the right for the restless solidarity of the mountain, slowly dragging himself forward.

Suddenly, his right hand touched nothing, then he was rolling endlessly down. Rocks pummeled him, and the earth peppered his face. Twigs tore at him, as he fell. He grasped for anything with his hands, clutching at rocks only to feel them pull loose.

He had to stop! In the giant darkness, wispy shrubs slipped through his fingers, as he clawed at the mountain, but still he slid down.

Gradually, he realized he was moving more slowly. His hands finally dug into soil, and he stopped. Was he at the bottom? He hadn't been moving long enough for that.

He laid his head against the earth, pressing his face into the soft dirt before cautiously raising himself and nestling into a crouch. Turning laboriously, he shifted his bruised body until he sat with his back to the mountain.

He gingerly felt along his limbs. Other than cuts and bruises from being tossed into and then ejected from what felt like a cement mixer, he was all right. Spitting dirt and debris from his mouth, he took a deep breath.

The inhalation stopped short. He heard a sound and sensed the presence of another living creature.

There was no moon to reflect or reveal, as the creature came boldly forward. Its warm nose touched his hand. He bit his tongue, tasting the salt of a silent cry.

It came closer, and he saw its eyes by their own luminescence. His heart pounded, and he pressed against the mountain, then he started laughing. It was squeaky at first, as he transitioned from fear, until he started guffawing in exuberant relief at seeing a plain, black-faced raccoon!

His friend scampered away, frightened by the noise. He'd been expecting a wildcat or something worse.

The laughter poured new strength into his tired, tense body. He struggled to his feet, shaking his legs to get the blood moving again. Leaning against the mountain, he looked out into the darkness that seemed friendlier than before and shouted, "I'm here! Do you hear me?"

"Hear me.... Hear me.... Hear me...." echoed the hills.

Light hovered over the mountaintops, as they reflected the approaching dawn. Dave rubbed his arms with sore hands, trying to stamp his feet enough to stir them without dislodging himself from his precarious haven on the ledge where he fell.

He looked up, as a strange new sound disturbed the morning air. The clattering, whirring wings of a helicopter investigated the mountain like a bumblebee perusing a flower.

Dave pulled off his parka and waved. The windmill machine chattered and roared, moving down the mountainside.

Dave waved frantically, his bruised arms feeling heavy. It was difficult raising them overhead.

Slowly, the noisy machine neared. It was so loud, he couldn't hear himself screaming. It hovered a short distance to the northeast, then skittered across the ravine to explore the other side.

He sobbed in frustration, waving harder. Surely, they could see the red badge of his parka. His lungs were bursting, as if he'd finished a long run. Was this like death, not being able to draw another breath?

The men in the helicopter checked with headquarters and were told to make one more pass down the mountain. Searchers on foot covered the trail thoroughly on the other side of the peak.

Slowly, the cumbersome bird ascended, preparing to flutter down one last time.

A tiny flash of red fluttered against the brown-gray granite and scrub oak, and the pilot moved toward it.

Dave watched them come closer, his arms wooden. He saw their faces, and his lips hurt when he smiled.

The men lowered a rope ladder., making the mountain shudder with the machine's vibration. Dave watched his way down, up, or out come closer.

The man at the top of the ladder gestured, while the pilot worked to keep the helicopter in position.

When the rope was only a foot overhead, he willed himself to jump. He cried out, as the force of gravity tried to reclaim him once he had the rope. Slowly, boy, machine, and man worked unevenly to meet.

Eventually, Dave felt the hard edge of the doorway, then strong arms hauled him aboard. The man slapped his back in encouragement, as he dragged his legs in behind him.

Conversation was impossible because of the noise, and Dave was glad. The men jokingly welcomed him, but his mind remained with the mountain. His aching body reminded him of a long night. He'd been a crazy kid, giving someone else the chance to play hero.

He closed his eyes and let himself drift into the blackness of his mind.

When he slowly opened them again, he saw the ground rising to meet them, as they landed.

Leaning over, he asked, "Hey, how about calling in a news report to KMFK?"

They smiled.

A FISHY TALE

Margreta Klassen

Joe Nixon's hands tightly grasped the steering wheel, as he maneuvered the car around the truck that lay gasping steam from its radiator on the side of the steep hill.

"Damn Mexicans and their trucks," he said. "They don't know the first thing about mechanics. Pee-uw! They stink!"

His wife looked up from the catalog she was reading on her phone. "Joe, for heaven's sake."

"They do. The trucks stink. The stuff they carry stinks. The people stink. The whole damn country smells to high heaven."

"Why do you come, then?"

"Because it's the only place to catch fish, and you know it."

"I sure get sick of hearing you gripe on the trip down."

The car weaved in and out of slow-moving vehicles climbing the tortuous hill. It barely got back in line before a careening bus whizzed past.

"Kee-rist! See what I mean? They drive like maniacs."

"You don't have to come down here. After all, you don't drive so great yourself."

"What d'ya mean, I don't drive so great? I never had an accident. Who got a ticket for speeding on the freeway?"

"Never mind who." She snapped her book shut. "Look." She pointed out the window.

The Pacific unfurled below the steep cliffs on their right, like a bolt of blue cloth edged with lacey foam. Tufts of cactus and sagebrush made a brown contrast on the hill above the road."

"It's prettier every time we come," she said.

"You're right. Look at those breakers. The tide's just right for perch to be biting. What d'ya say we take a quick spin down to the beach? I remember a dirt road along here someplace."

"Joe, you promised we'd drive straight through. You have reservations for a boat tomorrow."

"Well, OK, but that surf looks great. I can hear the line singin' out now. Half an hour, maybe?" He lifted one eyebrow and grinned at her.

"No. I'm tired. Sitting on the sandy beach in the wind sounds like my idea of nothing at all."

Frowning, he pressed his foot down on the accelerator. As the car's wheels spun dirt from the soft shoulder, an old woman driving a donkey shook her fist at them, then shrugged helplessly.

They arrived an hour later. After checking into the motel, they went out to dinner. They enjoyed eating at the small cafés where round Mexican women stood placidly patting fresh tortillas between their smooth palms.

The smell of the *masa*, corn flour ground in an ancient manner on a stone *metate*, drifted through the café screens. The screens had time-worn holes in them large enough for street urchins to push their faces through to sniff the savory goodness.

"That's the only smell in the whole blasted town that's any good," Joe said.

"I'm starved, Joe. Hurry and order."

"I'll have lobster. What do you want?"

A small, doe-eyed waitress stood near their table, smiling nervously, while Renay Nixon studied the menu.

"A combination plate, please," she told the waitress.

The shy girl bent her black head down, as she scribbled the order. *"Sí, Señora, y langouste por el Señor."*

"Never mind then double talk," Joe said. "Just bring the food and don't take all night."

"Joe, not so loud. I can't understand why you don't try to learn the language. We come so often."

"That's their problem. They like Yankee dollars, let 'em learn Yankee talk. We're their bread and butter."

They ate quickly and returned to the motel. Renay paused to look in an importer's window, where trays of turquoise and silver gleamed dully in the dim night. A single strand of pearls stood apart on a velvet cushion.

Joe continued walking. When he finally turned, he saw Renay standing half a block away. He took long strides to walk back.

"For Christ's sake, Renay. You were the one who was tired. I'm getting up early. Look all you want tomorrow while I'm on the boat."

He took her arm and walked her the two blocks back to their motel. The soft sounds of marimba came from the piano bar, and a gaudy neon sign flashed off and on above the entrance.

"Look, Joe." She tugged his arm. "There's Manuel."

"So?"

"I want to ask him about that bracelet I saw last time."

"For Pete's sake, not tonight."

"But...."

"Tomorrow."

She looked over her shoulder, as they walked to their room. The bar grew noisier, as it filled with tourists.

Since he didn't have an alarm clock, Joe stopped at the office and asked them to call him at 4:45. He and Renay went to bed at nine-thirty, while the mariachis beat a noisy lullaby, and glasses clinked in counterpoint.

Joe, tired from the drive, slept heavily.

He woke in a stupor when Renay shook him.

"Joe, wake up. They called. It's time to go."

He sat on the side of the bed, scratching himself. He stumbled around the room, pulling on his fishing clothes and gathering his gear.

When he opened the door, it was still dark outside. The patrons at the bar made merrier than before, and a blinking light momentarily lit the room. He saw Renay's red head motionless on the pillow and wondered how she heard the call, woke him, and went back to sleep so fast. The warm bed beckoned.

He closed the door quietly. As he passed the bar, he saw Manuel, Renay's friend, talking to an American who had trouble standing upright. As Joe watched, the man slowly slid off his seat.

The bar looked pleasant and warm, while the night air was brisk, but the thought of what liquor would feel like when the sea rolled the boat made him turn and walk toward town.

He entered the small *oficina* where Tomas, the fisherman, solicited.

Americans to try the fabulous fishing of Mexican waters. A young man dressed in faded khakis nodded off behind the battered desk.

"Hey, you. Wake up. When does the boat shove off?"

The Mexican's head rose slowly, and he looked at him in confusion. "Thee boat, *Señor*? What boat?"

"What boat? You stupid peon! The fishing boat at the marina! I have it chartered for five o'clock. Where is everyone?"

"But *Señor*, you are early. The boat, she does not leave until five."

"What the hell time do you think it is?"

"Four, *Señor*."

"You're joking."

"No, *Señor*. No joke. Thee boat leeves een wan 'our. Thees ees for sure."

Joe looked at the slight figure. He seemed to be telling the truth. He had to take the man's word for it, because he left his watch on the dresser in the motel. If it was only four, why had Renay wakened him so early?

He turned abruptly and strode across the street, where he pushed into an all-night café. Practically all the town's businesses were open all night, he saw, which meant more time to make money off the tourists.

After drinking two cups of what passed for "reel 'merican coffee" that tasted more like liquid distilled from old inner tubes. Joe saw several fishermen walking down the steep incline to the bay, where the fishing fleet lay like bobbing silhouettes at the beginning of morning.

An hour later, the boat was cruising off the outer islands. Joe caught several barracuda but nothing spectacular.

"What's the matter with the fish, Tomas?" he asked.

"Pretty soon, *Señor*. When eet ees time, he come."

"You mean even the fish keep you waiting in Mexico?"

"Ah, *Señor*, sometime thee feesh, he like thee siesta or maybe chase girl feesh." Shrugging, he smiled.

Joe leaned casually against the rail, as he trolled behind the boat. Suddenly, when his rod jerked hard, he whooped in delight.

The first surge caught him off balance, and he barely hung on. The monster came in like an Indianapolis racer and took off like the lead car in the Grand Prix.

The blue-green water churned into white foam, as the skipper backed the boat while Joe fought to regain his still-running line. Inch by inch, he reeled in the reluctant line, realizing he wasn't about to turn the opponent at the other end.

Joe, setting the drag on his reel even higher, worked harder. Sweat ran down his rough cheeks, until the cigarette clamped between his teeth was a soggy mass of chewed paper and tobacco.

The fish stopped momentarily. Joe took a few quick breaths, hastily wiping his hands on his pants, and the marathon among man, boat, and fish started up again. Which would outwit the other was hard to guess.

The Mexican skipper zigzagged skillfully ahead of the fish and ran obliquely to it to keep Joe's line taut. As they veered and twisted in a strange marine rhythm, Joe became conscious of the skipper's skill. He had to give those Mexicans credit. They could handle a boat better than anyone.

The fish sounded again, and Joe fell into the fighting chair, his legs quivering from tension.

Tomas wiped Joe's forehead with a soft cloth and offered a cold beer. Joe swilled it down quickly and handed it back, smiling at the boatman for the first time.

"Thanks, Man. This is what I call living."

"*Si, Señor.* You happy now?"

"You bet."

The fish must've taken time out for tactical meditation, because it surfaced madly. Joe reeled frantically, leaping back to his feet. He did a fast shuffle around the fantail, his hands high on the rod.

The fish acted like a troupe of Italian acrobats, twisting, jumping, and doing loop-the-loops as it fought for freedom.

When the fish broke water, Tomas shouted, "*Papagallo, Señor. Papagallo!*"

Joe gasped, biting his lip with excitement. That was the game-cock of the Pacific, a roosterfish. He'd heard of them but never saw one before, and now he had one at the end of his line.

It sizzled through the water, churning a desperate wake. Joe kept expecting the heavy tackle to break under the strain. Twice he had the fish alongside the boat, and Tomas leaned precariously over the side with the gaff. Their wary prey wasn't ready to give up yet. With a swirl and splash, it plunged under the boat and disappeared.

It took thirty minutes for Joe to land the iridescent green and silver fighter. When Tomas finally laid it at Joe's feet, he marveled at its beauty. The pronounced dorsal fin truly resembled a cock's tail, while the forward fin boasted spiny fingers that waved languidly, as the fish cruised under the surface, stiffened into a cockscomb when the fish was in danger.

Tomas grinned broadly at Joe, who felt a sudden kinship with the men who were so much a part of the sea and its bounty. Money wasn't important out there. He stretched his aching legs, glancing rue-fully at the blisters on his calloused hands. He felt good.

When the boat moored at the dock, Joe felt happy and bois-terous and tried to give Tomas a big tip.

"No, *Señor*. You hire the boat. I go weeth eet. *Muchas gra-cias.*"

Joe looked at the money and shoved it back into his pocket be-fore offering his hand. "How do you say it? Moochas grass-ee-as?"

"*Sí, Señor. Por nada.*"

"*Sí, Señor. Por nada.*"

Joe whistled tuneless, as he trudged up the hill, followed by a Mexican pushing the fish in a small wooden cart. The smell of a sewer blew into his face, but he didn't wrinkle his nose.

"Ice it down," he told the man. "I want my wife to see this lit-tle gem."

The man touched his fingers to his cap and disappeared into the dark opening of a wooden structure built into the hillside. A large sign that seemed to support the roof proclaimed, *Smoked Fish, Ice....*

Joe walked faster, as he approached the motel, trying not to run. What a day it was! He went inside and thrust open the door to their room.

"The fisherman cometh!" he proclaimed. "Or something like that. I'm back."

Gloomy silence answered him. His smile faded, as he realized Renay wasn't there. The bed was smooth and unwrinkled, and he wondered if he had the wrong room. He walked out to inquire at the office.

"No, *Señor*. The *Señora* did not leave a message."

She's probably shopping, he thought. *She knows I'd be back around two. Damn all those shops and their female gee-gaws.*

He stopped at the first hole-in-the-wall hung with baskets of various shapes and sizes. His temper rose when he bumped his head against a reed monkey swinging lazily from the entrance arch.

"You seen an American woman, red hair, pretty?"

"No, *Señor*. Wanna buy a basket? *Señoras* like baskets. We got beeg ones or leetle ones. How about two?"

"I don't need any baskets. I'm looking for my wife." He walked away, as the proprietor arranged an assortment of baskets, so the American could better appreciate their lopsided craftsmanship.

Around him, *chamacos* chorused, "Choo'n gum, Meester. Wanna shine?"

He brushed them aside like a flurry of gnats and walked into a small dress shop that seemed empty.

"Tortillas! Awk! Tortillas and beer, *Señor*."

He whirled, looking for the source of the raucous voice. An elderly man slipped silently from behind a floral curtain at the back of the shop.

"That's what he likes to eat, *Señor*. May I be of assistance?"

"That's what who likes to eat?"

"My friend, El Perico." He pointed at a perch in the dim corner.

"Awk! Tortillas! Tortillas and beer!" The green parrot pressed its beak against its feathers and regarded Joe with one beady eye. Joe glared back and turned to the old man.

"Yes, you can help. I'm looking for my wife. She's about so tall." He held one hand to his shoulder. "Her hair is red."

"Ah, *si, pela roja. Muy simpatico.* She ees your wife?"

"You've seen her?"

"*Si, Señor.* She was here two hours ago. She bought a mantilla for her pretty hair."

"Did she say where she was going next?"

"She said something about an appointment. I cannot remember the place."

"Awk! Tortillas!"

Joe, glancing at the bird with exasperation, tossed a crumpled bill on the glass counter. "Buy your friend a tortilla."

The silver-haired man regarded the bird with a faint smile and waved the money at it, as the American left. "Ah, *perico.* The Americans are always in such --a hurry, in more ways than one."

"Awk! Tortillas!"

"*Si, mi amigo.* One for you and two for me."

Joe stood on the curb. Dust swirled around his feet, as a taxi screeched.

Joe stood on the curb. Dust swirled around his feet, as a taxi screeched past on two wheels, blasting its horn. The town wasn't big enough for Renay to disappear. She had to be somewhere within a mile radius. The glow of his morning's conquest faded rapidly.

"Want to buy a watch, *Señor?*"

Joe almost shouted at the man, then reconsidered. "Say, Buddy, you see a red-haired *señora* around here anywhere?"

"Thees ees a very fine watch, *Señor.*"

"I don't need a watch. I'm trying to find my wife. Have you seen her?"

"*Si, Señor.* She go to Manuel's, then the ice house."

"Manuel's? Of course. Why didn't I think of that first? Did you say the ice house?"

"*Sí, Señor.* You sure you don' want to buy a watch?"

"Yeah, I'm sure." He flipped a coin at the man, and it disappeared without the man moving perceptibly.

As Joe hurried toward Manuel's, he heard the pitch being given to the next tourist.

"Wanna buy a watch, *Señor?* Reel Swees watch, very nice."

The door tinkled musically, as Joe opened it to enter the plush interior. Manuel's wasn't an ordinary shop. Here, Americans bought Austrian cashmere, French perfume, fine jewelry, and expensive cloth.

"May I help you?"

Joe looked at the saleswoman, a very elegant Mexican. Her hair was pulled smoothly back into a classic style, and her ancestry spoke of Spanish rather than Indian heritage. It was clear that Manuel's had class.

"I'm looking for *Señora* Nixon. You've seen her, haven't you?"

"Yes, *Señor.* She's been here many times."

"I mean today, the last couple of hours."

"I believe she was here very early this morning, *Señor.* Manuel assisted her with her purchases. Would you like to speak with him?"

"No, thanks. She's probably back at the motel, and I missed her. Thanks again."

Somehow, Joe walked back to the motel. The roosterfish had lost some of its savor. He wished Renay was there to greet him, as the boat docked.

She was combing her hair when he walked in. "Where have you been, Joe? I waited for you at the dock."

"What do you mean, where have I been? I've been looking all over town for you."

"Why...I...."

"You know I like you to be waiting when I come in."

"I'm sorry, Joe. Don't be mad." She stood and curved her body against his. The smell of her hair filled his nostrils, and he wasn't angry anymore.

The long line of cars moved slowly across the border. Crisply tailored customs men bent over to peer inside each car.

"Where were you born? What did you buy? Do you have any liquor?"

They asked standard questions before waving tired tourists on their way. Joe nosed his car into line. The customs officer began his interrogation, but he added an extra question.

"What was the purpose of your trip to Mexico?"

"I was after the big fish, and I caught him. Yes, Sir, I got thirty-five pounds of *papagallo*."

The officer smiled. "Is that so? I've never seen one of those. Would you mind pulling over to the side?"

Renay frowned at Joe. "Now look what you did with your bragging. We'll be here for hours."

"For Pete's sake," he said. "Half the fun of catching a fish is showing it to people. The guy's never seen a *papagallo*. I'll give him a thrill.'

"Well, I don't like it, and I wish you'd kept your mouth shut."

The customs officer beckoned another driver to take Joe's place in the slow-moving line, then walked back to where Joe opened his trunk. He helped Joe lifted out the ice chest and set it on the ground. Renay got out and walked toward the customs station.

"Wait'll you see this, Officer," Joe said. "It's different from any fish you've seen. I'll bet you a cigar."

The officer threw open the chest, and the fish, even in death, was magnificent. The proud cock's comb sprouted defiantly from its head.

"Looks at those colors," Joe said. "Aren't they something?"

"You can say that again. That silvery green gleams like pearls." The customs officer reached down to touch the fish.

Something glistened between the fish and the ice. Brushing away the chipped ice, he held up the object to Joe's amazed gaze.

"I thought these came only in oysters," the customs man said sarcastically.

"What the hell? How did...?"

"Come on, Mister. You have some explaining to do."

Joe shook his head in disbelief, as they entered the building. Another officer had a firm grip on Renay's arm, and she screamed at him.

"You and your lousy fish!" she shouted. "You're always bragging. I never had trouble until you bragged about your lousy fish!"

CHAPTER 7

MR. CARVER'S DREAM

Ricardo Rodriguez

June 17, 1949, was a bright, sunny day in Jasper, just outside of Birmingham, Alabama. The temperature was warm, birds chirped, and a rooster crowed. Families put breakfast on their tables.

A man rode his horse across a field as if he were being chased. He lost control and fell off, cracking his head and knocking him unconscious.

Several minutes later, he was found by a few of his workers and was carried to his large home, where they placed him on a bed. One worker quickly called the town doctor and told him to come right away. Others wrapped ice in rags and placed the bundle on his bruise.

Fifteen minutes later, the doctor arrived and was led into the room.

A young maid told the doctor, "There goes Mr. Carver

The doctor found the man's vital signs were all right, so he woke him with smelling salts.

Mr. Carver seemed puzzled to find himself lying on a large bed in a big bedroom, being tended by a Black doctor and two young White women in maid's outfits.

"What am I doing here?" he asked. "What are y'all doing to me?"

"Mr. Carver," a maid said, "we're trying to take care of that wound on your head. You fell off your horse, and we called Dr. Jones."

"Who am I that y'all are taking care of me? I can't remember a thing."

The maids whispered together.

"Oh, Lord," one said, "he must've hit his head really hard."

The other maid turned to him. "Well, Sir, your name is Nathaniel Carver, and you're married to a wonderful wife named Claudia. You have two beautiful children named Nathaniel Junior and Joanna. You're one of the richest men in all Alabama."

"I am? I'm Black!"

"Of course, you are, Sir."

The others in the room exchanged worried glances.

"Mr. Carver," Dr. Jones said, "you need rest."

The maids and the doctor left the room, closing the door behind them to gather in the hall.

"It's worse than we thought," one maid said. "We must send for Mrs. Carver. He isn't doing well."

Mr. Carver, feeling a bit dizzy, fell asleep quickly. While he slept, he twitched and moaned, and he began perspiring.

A maid sent Mr. Carver's driver to fetch Mrs. Carver, who was having breakfast at the local country club with her friends.

The driver arrived at the country club and ran to the hostess. "Please find Mrs. Carver. It's urgent."

Moments later, Mrs. Carver came through the doorway. "What's going on?"

"Hurry, Ma'am. It's Mr. Carver. He fell off his horse and bumped his head pretty badly."

She got into the car, and they drove to the house. As soon as they arrived, she was greeted by Dr. Jones and the maids.

The doctor took her aside. "Mrs. Carver, your husband hit his head pretty hard, and he seems to have some memory loss."

"Memory loss?"

"Yes, but with plenty of rest, he'll be all right." He walked toward the door.

"Thank you very much, Dr. Jones. I'll be in touch if I need you."

Mr. Carver opened his eyes and found himself in a strange bedroom. He jumped out of bed, wondering where he was.

Mrs. Carver walked in through the bedroom door. "Nathaniel, you should be in bed. Dr. Jones said you need rest."

"Are you my wife, Claudia?"

"Nathaniel Carver! Have you lost your mind?"

"I think so." He stared out the window at the huge estate.

"Would you like me to call Dr. Jones again? He said to call if I had any concerns."

"No. There's no need to call him. You should tell me a few things about myself and our family. Maybe that will help my memory."

"Your name is Nathaniel Carver. I'm your wife, Claudia, of fourteen years. We have two wonderful children. Nathaniel Junior is twelve, and Joanna is nine. We own one of the biggest tire-manufacturing companies in the country, called Carver Tires. That's why you're one of the richest men in the South."

Puzzled, he frowned. "How is it that we have White people working for us? Don't the Blacks usually work for the Whites?

"Oh, Lord, no. Whites have always worked for us. Well, they have ever since we brought them over from Europe."

"We brought Whites here from Europe?"

She nodded. "Yes. Our ancestors did that."

"Why?"

"As far as I know, when our ancestors first arrived here, there were already some natives, but our ancestors wanted it all for themselves, so they went to Europe and lied to the Whites, promising if they came here to help us cultivate and build it up, they would be paid in free land and other favors. That was a long time ago, though, and the situation is much better for the Whites now. At least they aren't slaves anymore."

"Well, I guess that's better."

"We should take a ride around town to see if that jogs your memory."

They changed clothes, went downstairs, and called for their driver. When the car was ready, they went outside, where the driver helped both of them in.

John, the driver, sat behind the wheel and drove off. "Is there anywhere in particular y'all would like to go?"

"Oh, no, John," Mrs. Carver replied. "Just drive."

"Yes, Ma'am."

Nathaniel quickly noticed that all the businesses were owned by Blacks, and Whites were allowed to enter only through the back.

"Why do some places have signs that read *Blacks Only—Whites in the back?*"

"I really don't know. That's the way it's always been."

"I don't think that's fair. They're people just like us."

"It's been that way a long time. There's no point trying to change it. Like I said before, at least they aren't slaves anymore. Nathaniel, don't worry about that. We need to bring back your memory. Let's visit the factory.

"John, take us to the factory."

"Yes, Ma'am."

A few minutes later, they arrived at a large manufacturing plant. Nathaniel stared in awe, which worried her a little.

She took his hand, as they left the car. "Come on. Let me show you around."

As they walked through the facility and looked at the production lines, they met several managers along the way. Mrs. Carver had to explain to them all what happened, so she gathered them in the office, while Nathaniel continued walking around on his own.

The workers greeted him kindly. He was clearly well liked.

"Good afternoon, Mr. Carver," one said. "How are you doing today? You don't look quite like yourself."

"Well, Young Man, I'm doing just fine. I had a little accident, but I'm much better. Thanks for asking."

"You're welcome, Sir." He returned to work.

Nathaniel continued his walk, trying to become familiar with the surroundings.

"Listen up, Folks," Mrs. Carver told the assembled staff. "I don't know if any of y'all have heard, but Mr. Carver was in a terrible accident. He fell off his horse and struck his head hard enough to cause memory loss. I'll need all of you to help see if we can get his memory back."

"If he has some memory loss," one manager joked, "maybe I should tell him I haven't had a raise in a while." After the laughter died down, he added, "Seriously, Mrs. Carver, we'll do whatever it takes to make him better."

"Thank you. Now y'all get back to work. Mr. Walker, come with me. We'll talk to my husband and see if he remembers you."

They went down to the production floor and found Mr. Carver wandering around, examining the plant with interest.

"Nathaniel, here's our plant manager, Mr. Mike Walker," Claudia said.

"You remember Mike, don't you?"

"Hi, Mr. Carver," Mike said. "I'm sorry about your accident. I hope you're feeling OK."

"I feel OK, Mr.... I'm sorry. What was your name again?"

"No problem. I'm Michael Walker, but you can call me Mike. I've been running your plant for a little over ten years now. I started on the floor, but you saw my potential and promoted me. You made me into the man I am today. I really appreciate that, Sir."

"That's good to hear, Son. Can I ask you a question?"

"Of course. What's on your mind?"

"How come there are only Blacks working here? Are there no Whites who might be interested in these jobs?"

Mike looked at Mrs. Carver in amazement. She gave him a look that indicated not to take the question too seriously.

"Well, Sir, since you started the company, and since I've been here, we've never had anyone who wasn't Black in this plant. There are some pretty sophisticated machines, and we don't know if Whites are capable of running them."

"Exactly! You don't know if they're capable. That needs to change, Mr. Walker."

"Of course, Sir. As soon as there's an opening, I'll make sure that happens."

Mr. Carver walked away. "Come on, Honey. All this walking has made me hungry."

"Coming!" She looked at Mike. "You see what I'm saying? He's lost his mind!"

Mike shook his head, a puzzled frown on his face. As Mrs. Carver walked away, he called, "Have a great day, Mr. and Mrs. Carver. Sir, I hope you feel better!"

"Thank you, Mr. Walker, but I already feel great. Have a good day."

They returned to the car. John held the door for them, and they thanked him, as they got in.

"You're welcome," John said. "Where would you like to go next, Ma'am?"

"Nathaniel's hungry, so take us to our favorite restaurant."

"Yes, Ma'am."

Ten minutes later, they arrived at Grandma Mabel's Home Cooking, known throughout the South for its authentic Southern dishes. Mr. Carver's favorite was shrimp and grits with cornbread and a glass of Southern iced tea.

When they walked in, the hostess greeted them immediately.

"Hello, Mr. and Mrs. Carver," she said. "Come with me, and I'll take you to your table." She led them to their usual table, then a waitress arrived.

"How are y'all doing today, Mr. and Mrs. Carver?" she asked. "Sorry for the wait."

"Oh, no, Sugar," Mrs. Carver said. "We didn't wait long." She smiled. "We'll have our usual. Thank you."

"Coming right up."

After the waitress left, Mr. Carver asked, "Honey, when do the children get out of school?"

"They come home tomorrow from school, then they'll start summer vacation." Seeing his confusion, she added, "You must not remember they attend Jefferson Academy, which is about three hours away. That's why they come home only on weekends, holidays, or for the summer."

"Why so far away?"

"It's the most-prestigious school for the gifted and privileged, like our children," she said with pride.

"Wow. That's great. I can't wait to see them."

"I'm sure they'll be excited to see you, too, especially after your accident."

The waitress brought their meals. They thanked her, and she said, "You're very welcome. Enjoy your meals."

Mr. Carver took a bite., "Umm, umm! I definitely remember this. My God, how I've missed this."

They giggled.

"Of course, you do," she replied. "How can you forget the best plate of shrimp and grits in the whole South?"

Grandma Mabel walked up to their table.

"Hello, Mrs. Mabel," Mrs. Carver said. "What a pleasure to see you here. How are you?"

"I'm doing fine considering my age. I turned eighty-one not long ago," she added with pride.

"That's wonderful, Mrs. Mabel. Happy birthday! What brings you out here? It's been awhile since I last saw you."

"When you get to be my age, you don't get out much, but when I heard about Nathaniel's accident, and I found y'all were here, I had them bring me over to see how you're doing."

"I'm doing fine, Mrs. Mabel," Mr. Carver said. "I'm having trouble remembering some things, but I definitely remember these shrimp and grits. This is delicious!"

She smiled. "I know, Nathaniel. Ever since you were a little boy, that's been your favorite dish."

"Mrs. Mabel has known your family since you were a boy," his wife added. "That's why she's the only one in town who can call you by your first name. Everyone else calls you Mr. Carver."

"I'll let you folks enjoy your meal," Mrs. Mabel said. "I'll be heading home for some rest."

"Thank you, Mrs. Mabel," Mrs. Carver said.

"Yes," Mr. Carver added. "Thank you for coming to see me."

"No problem, Nathaniel. You take care of yourself and stay away from those horses!" She smiled and walked toward the door.

"That Mrs. Mabel is such a sweet old lady to come out here to see how I'm doing," Mr. Carver said.

"She sure is. Now let's eat before this food gets cold."

They discussed old times and how they met, laughing and having a good time while they ate. Shortly after they finished, they left the restaurant, and John held the car doors for them to enter.

"John, could you please just take us home?" Mrs. Carver asked. "It's been a long day."

Several minutes later, they arrived at their home, and John opened the doors for them. Mrs. Carver got out first and walked inside. Mr. Carver stood beside the car, marveling at the beautiful home and grounds.

"Isn't life wonderful?" he asked, sighing.

"Will you get in here, Nathaniel Carver?" his wife called from the front door. "We've got some celebrating to do!"

She ordered a maid to bring a bottle of wine, and she scurried off. Mr. Carver followed Mrs. Carver inside.

"Am I dreaming?" he asked. "If this is a dream, please don't wake me."

He laughed and took the glass of wine the maid brought.

"Stop being silly," Mrs. Carver said. "Let's dance."

She put on their favorite record, and they danced and kissed.

"Claudia Carver, I love you so much," he said.

"Nathaniel Carver, I love you more, and I'm glad you're feeling better."

They kissed passionately, then she abruptly pulled away. "I have a great idea. Let's have our closest friends come over with their children. The kids will be back tomorrow afternoon."

"OK," he said. "Let's do it!"

They danced and drank more wine.

When both of them felt tired, they decided to go to bed. Once in the bedroom, Mrs. Carver went into the master bath, brushed her teeth, and put on her nightgown.

"Honey, aren't you gonna brush your teeth?" she asked.

He didn't reply.

"Honey?" She walked into the bedroom and found him on his side of the
bed, asleep with his shirt off, although he still wore his pants and socks. She undressed him while he slept. The wine must have made him so sleepy.

He rolled over, and she covered him with a blanket. Going to her side of the bed, she settled under the covers and said softly, "What a day." She turned off the light.

"No, no, no! Stop! No!"

Startled, she turned on the light and saw her husband talking in his sleep.

"No, no, stop! No!"

"Nathaniel," she said, shaking him lightly.

He turned over, mumbled something, and started snoring.

"It must've been all that wine," she said, turning off the light and going back to sleep.

In the morning, Mrs. Carver opened her eyes and said, "Good morning, Honey. Rise and shine." She snuggled against him.

He slowly opened his eyes. "Good morning," he said, smiling.

"Do you remember having a bad dream last night?"

"No, but my head is pounding from all the wine last night. Why?"

"Oh, nothing. It's no big deal. Let's hurry and get ready. We have a big day ahead."

They washed, and as they dressed, she said, "I sure am hungry. I can smell breakfast already. We should give you something for that headache."

"Yes, please." Groaning, he held his head in his hands.

They walked into the dining room, sat down, and were served by the maids.

"Could you please bring some aspirin for Mr. Carver?" Mrs. Carver asked. "He has a terrible headache."

"Right away, Mrs. Carver." The maid left the room and returned a moment later with a glass of water and two aspirin. "Here you go, Mr. Carver. Hope you feel better."

"Thank you very much." He popped the aspirin into his mouth and swallowed them with water. "Now I'm ready to eat this wonderful breakfast."

They ate eggs, bacon, ham, sausage, toast, hash browns, and orange juice. The maids were very attentive to their needs, and Mr. Carver was impressed. He decided to thank them personally.

After breakfast, he called the staff into the dining room. "I don't know if I ever said this before, but I know I speak for Claudia and myself when I say thank you for all the hard work you do. We appreciate it."

"You're welcome!" they chorused, although a few seemed shocked.

Mr. Carver, seeing their expressions, realized that was probably the first time in all the years they worked for him that he showed true appreciation. "I know this may seem like a dream, but I think the accident made me realize a lot of things. I've seen some problems around here, and I promise things will change for the better. We're having a feast tonight, and we're gonna need y'all here, but after that, you can take the rest of the weekend off. Yes, your time will be paid. I'll put a little extra something in your pay so you can have a good time with your families."

They stood like statues, unable to believe what he just said.

"I'm sorry, Mr. Carver," one finally asked, "but is this a joke?"

"No." He smiled. "I know it seems unreal, but it's not. If y'all want to have the rest of the weekend off, y'all better start cleaning up and preparing for tonight." He laughed.

"Yes, Sir!" a maid said. "Thank you so much!"

Mrs. Carver, pleased by this, went to sit on her husband's lap. "You know, I love the new you. You're much kinder and sweeter. I can't wait till the kids and our friends meet the new Mr. Carver."

"I appreciate that."

She leaned in to kiss him.

"It's a good thing I had that accident. I feel really good right now."

"OK. We have to go, though. John's waiting for us."

They reluctantly walked to the car, where John held the doors for them. He helped Mrs. Carver in first, then offered his hand to Mr. Carver.

"No, thanks, John. I can handle it."

They shared a smile.

"Yes, Sir."

As John got in the car, Mrs. Carver said, "John, I need a new dress. Nathaniel needs a new suit, something really nice."

"I know a great place to take you in Birmingham."

As John drove off, the couple sat back and discussed how excited they were to see their kids again and about the party.

"Honey, it's not very important," he said, "but I've been meaning to ask how Mrs. Mabel found out about my accident."

"Honey, news travels fast. You have to understand that you're a very respected, powerful person in this community, even in the whole South."

That made him feel good. "I'm truly honored by that. Thanks."

They talked and enjoyed the view during the thirty-minute drive into Birmingham.

John stopped in front of a new store neither of them knew, because it was located in a neighborhood they hadn't visited before—a very poor White neighborhood.

"Why are we here with all these poor people?" Mrs. Carver asked.

"I'm sorry, Mrs. Carver, but I figured that since the accident, Mr. Carver has changed, so maybe I should've asked. It's a shop owned by my great-uncle who came from Italy not long ago. I can take you to the usual place if you prefer."

"Hold up, John," Mr. Carver said, staring at a fine suit he saw in the shop window. "Claudia, Honey, we should give it a chance."

"Nathaniel, you don't remember, but we would never have come to a place like this in the past."

"Why? 'Cause they're poor, or 'cause they're White, or 'cause some might think they're beneath us? I don't see that right now. All I see is a beautiful suit I like."

Looking at the store, she noticed a lovely dress in the window. "Maybe you're right. We'll give it a chance."

John nervously opened the car door, then he walked ahead and opened the shop door for them. He introduced them to his great-uncle, who'd been in America for only one year. He was well-known in Italy as one of the finest tailors in Florence.

"Welcome, Mr. and Mrs. Carver. My name is Antonio Fiorini, but please just call me Antonio. It's a pleasure to finally meet you."

"Thank you," Mrs. Carver replied. "It's a pleasure to meet you, too."

"Thank you," Mr. Carver said. "I'm pleased to meet you, but please call me Nathaniel."

The two men shook hands.

"So, Antonio, when you said finally meet us, what did you mean?" he asked.

"I've been trying to convince John to bring you here for a long time, but because of the situation...."

"I understand," Mr. Carver said. "You know what? We're here now, so let's get down to business."

"Of course, Sir." He walked toward the back. "Excuse me. I'll be right back."

He returned with some of the finest cloth either of them had ever seen.

"What do you think?" Antonio asked. "Do you like it?"

"Like it!" Mrs. Carver exclaimed. "Oh, my God, I love it!"

Antonio showed Mr. Carver the material for his suit, and he loved it, too.

"Let me take your measurements," Antonio said, "and I'll have these things ready this afternoon."

"Really?" Mr. Carver asked.

"Of course. I know you have a special party tonight. You can send John
back this afternoon, and they'll definitely be ready."

"We really appreciate that," Mr. Carver said. "I didn't think something this beautiful could be finished so fast." He shook Antonio's hand again. "I'd like you to join us tonight."

"Nathaniel," his wife asked, "are you sure?"

"Of course, I am."

"I don't know, Mr. Carver," Antonio said nervously. "You know how things are...."

"Yes, Nathaniel," Mrs. Carver said. "You know how things are. Maybe we could talk to our friends first and see what they think."

"I know how it is," he said, "and it needs to change. That change starts with us, and it starts today. How long are we supposed to wait? What if no one ever says anything or tries to fix this problem? It *is* a problem." He look at Antonio. "I won't take no for an answer. I'll see you there tonight, right?"

"OK, Mr. Carver. If you insist. Let's get these measurements, so I can start work."

When the measurements were finished, Mr. Carver said, "Thank you very much, Antonio. We'll see you tonight. I'll have John sent back to pick up the clothes."

"Yes, Mr. Carver. You're very welcome. I'll see you tonight."

John opened the door, as they left the shop, and they waved good-bye to Antonio.

"That Mr. Fiorini is such a nice man," Mr. Carver told his wife.

"He is, but do you think that's a good idea, inviting him over tonight?"

"Yes, I do, and I don't care what anyone thinks. Where do we go next?"

"We have to visit Johnson's, which is where we usually buy our clothing, but we'll just get something for the kids." She spoke to John. "Take us there next, please."

"Right away, Ma'am." As he drove toward the city, he said, "I'm really sorry about that. I should've asked you first before I brought y'all here."

"No need to apologize, John," Mr. Carver said. "I'm glad you did." He turned to his wife. "You know, Honey, I'm starting to open my eyes, and I'll figure out something and tell you later. Right now, let's focus on the kids and the party."

"Of course, Honey."

Ten minutes later, they arrived at Johnson's, a store they frequented when they needed clothing.

"We're here, Nathaniel," Mrs. Carver said.

"Honey, would it be OK for you to go in and grab the things for the kids? I'll wait here for you and talk to John."

"Are you sure?"

"Don't worry, Mrs. Carver," John said. "I'll take good care of him." He chuckled.

Mrs. Carver laughed. "Oh, I know. I'll try to make this quick."

John got out and opened the door for her, then he got back into the car.

Mrs. Carver knew exactly where to go to find children's clothing, so she shopped quickly and went directly to the register to pay and leave. She didn't want her husband alone with John for too long, even though she knew it would be all right.

She paid and walked toward the door when someone called her name. She turned to see Harold Johnson, the owner.

"How are you doing?" he asked. "How's Mr. Carver? I heard about his accident."

"I'm fine, and he's doing much better, other than having trouble remembering some things."

They continued speaking while a commotion started outside.

Mr. Carver, speaking with John. saw two policemen harassing two young White boys. He got out of the car and ran over.

"Hey! What are you doing to those boys?" he demanded.

"Mr. Carver?" one asked, recognizing him immediately. "We ain't doin' nothin' to these boys. We're just askin' them what they're doin' around here. They don't belong in this neighborhood, and they know it."

"We ain't done nothin', Mr. Carver," one boy said. "Me and my brother are just lookin' for work."

An officer grabbed his shirt. "Shut up, Boy, or you're gonna get arrested."

"Let these boys go right now!" Mr. Carver snapped. "You heard them. They aren't doing anything wrong. They're just looking for work." He looked at the boys. "If you're looking for work, I can get you jobs at my factory. Do you know where it is?"

"Yes, Sir!" they chorused.

Mr. Carver nodded approvingly. "Come over on Monday. Ask for Mike Walker, my plant manager, and tell him I sent you."

"Thank you, Mr. Carver!" they said.

"You're welcome. Run along now. I'll take care of the rest."

They ran off.

John ran into the store to find Mrs. Carver. "Please come quickly. It's Mr. Carver!"

"Oh, God, Harold. I have to go. I'll see you at the party tonight."

"See you then, Mrs. Carver."

She ran outside and said, "Nathaniel, what's going on?"

"Oh, nothing. I was just telling these fine officers they shouldn't harass innocent people no matter what color they are."

"You don't know if they were doing something they shouldn't," she replied.

"I do know. I was a witness to the whole situation, right, Officers?"

The two officers stood quietly.

"Sorry, Officers," Mrs. Carver said. "My husband suffered an accident yesterday."

"Yes, Ma'am," one said. "We heard."

"I'd like to remind you two," Mr. Carver said, "that no one gets to choose the color he's born with. God made him that way no matter how we might feel about it."

"Yes, Sir," the same officer said. "You're absolutely right. It won't happen again. Y'all have a great rest of your day."

The two policemen walked off.

Mrs. Carver took her husband's hand. "Come on. Let's go home before you get into trouble."

"Trouble? Why? I'm speaking the truth."

"Come on. Let's just go. John, please take us home."

"Right away, Ma'am." He held the door for them, then got behind the wheel and drove back to the house.

"Let's just relax for a while at home," Mrs. Carver said, "and wait for the kids. They'll be home soon."

"I can't wait to see them."

Once they were home, Mr. Carver decided to sit on the porch, while Mrs. Carver walked inside. She returned a moment later.

"Nathaniel, are you OK?" she asked.

"Yes, I'm fine. I just want to sit out here awhile and think."

"I'll go inside for a few minutes, then I'll join you."

"OK." He sat on the porch swing, lost in thought.

Ten minutes later, Mrs. Carver came out and sat beside him, holding his hand. "Nathaniel, I know you want to help, but you have to give it some time. Do things little by little."

"Time? Little by little? You mean we should keep ignoring the fact that people are treated badly based on the color of their skin or their income? Did we choose our own color? We both know that's wrong, and I want to do something about it. I don't want to give it more time."

"You're absolutely right, but it won't be easy. A lot of people will disagree, including our family and friends."

"I know, but like you told me, I'm powerful. I'm respected in this community. It shouldn't cause that much of a problem."

"Whatever plan you come up with, the first thing you need to do is pray to God and ask Him for guidance in such a delicate situation."

"That's exactly what I'll do."

"Just remember the children will be home soon, and I don't want them seeing you all upset."

Walking into the house, he picked up a Bible. Mrs. Carver remained outside to enjoy the weather.

Two hours later, Mr. Carver returned to the porch with a smile. "I know exactly what I want to do."

"That's great, Honey, but let's discuss it later. The kids are here."

He turned and saw the kids waving from a car approaching the house. They were excited to see their parents again, but it was also the beginning of summer vacation. When the car pulled up in front of the house, they ran out to hug their parents.

"You guys must be hungry," Mrs. Carver said. "Go inside and get out of those clothes. I'll have them prepare something to eat, then later we'll get ready for the party tonight."

"Party?" the kids asked, excited.

She smiled. "Yes, party. I'll explain later. Go inside and change."

They ran upstairs to their rooms to change.

"They won't know anything about all this," she told her husband. "Let me explain what happened to you."

"Of course, Honey."

She went inside and waited for the kids to come down. When they clattered down the stairs, she called them into the living room and told them to sit down.

"I have something to tell both of you," she began, "but you don't have to worry. Everything is fine."

"What is it, Mom?" Junior asked.

"Your dad had an accident."

"Accident? We just saw him outside. He looks fine."

"Yeah, Mom," Joanna added. "He looked fine to me, too."

She nodded. "Physically, he's fine, but he fell off his horse and bumped his head badly. He lost his memory."

"He doesn't remember us?" Junior became worried.

"No, he doesn't, but don't feel bad. He didn't remember me, either. If you're around him, and he says something that seems weird, don't pay too much you're around him, and he says something that seems weird, don't pay too much attention. I think having you around will really help him remember."

"OK," Joanna said.

"OK, Mom," Junior said. "We understand."

They went outside together, where they talked about school and how excited they were about summer vacation.

Half an hour later, Mrs. Carver said, "OK, we have to get ready. John should be back any minute with our clothes."

She sent the kids to their rooms to shower and change into new clothes for the party, and they left. A few minutes later, John arrived with clothing for Mr. and Mrs. Carver.

The adults went inside to prepare. While they were dressing, Mrs. Carver asked, "Honey, have you thought of a good plan? You said you know what you want to do."

"Yeah, but you'll have to wait until later, when I'll make an announcement in front of everyone."

"That's great, Honey, but we need to hurry. Our guests are arriving."

They hurried downstairs. She called to the kids, "Come on, Kids! Our guests are here!"

Once they were downstairs, they greeted their guests, including their children. As conversation ensued, Mr. and Mrs. Carver waited for the last guests to arrive, so he could make his big announcement.

Finally, all the guests were there except Mr. Fiorini.

"Excuse me, Everyone!" Mrs. Carver said. "First of all, I'd like to thank you for coming. As you know, Nathaniel had a little accident, but it was a blessing in disguise. I'll let him take over now."

They applauded, and Mr. Carver said, "Oh, come on. Y'all don't have to clap for me."

They stopped and waited.

"We're just glad you're alive and well," someone said. "It could've been much worse."

"Yes," he replied. "I'm definitely happy to be alive and well. All of y'all know I had an accident, but most of you don't know I lost my memory. Don't feel bad, but I don't remember any of you. However, although I lost my memory, I gained something else."

"Well, Mr. Carver," said the man who spoke earlier, "then let me introduce myself. I'm Edward Turner, a judge in the city of Birmingham, and I'd like to know just what you gained."

"Empathy, mercy, and compassion for people who, by no fault of their own, have been turned away or hated or worse." He suddenly had their full attention.

In the brief silence came a knock at the door, which the butler answered. A moment later, the butler came into the room.

"Excuse me, Mr. Carver. Your final guest of the night is here."

The others were shocked at who came in.

"Welcome, Mr. Fiorini," Mr. Carver said.

"Who is this man?" Judge Turner said. "Why is he here? I know you lost your memory, but let me remind you that we don't mix with these people."

"I knew this was a bad idea, Mr. Carver," Mr. Fiorini said. "I'll leave. I'm sorry for ruining your party."

"No. You stay right here," Mr. Carver said.

"He's right," the judge said. "He should leave, so we can continue our party. Then you can tell us what you were going to say."

"That's exactly what I was getting to. I plan to run for Governor of the State of Alabama. Eventually, I'll run for President. I want to ensure that all men, women, and children are treated equally."

"How do you plan to do that?" Judge Turner asked. "Don't you know that's impossible? Oh. I forgot about your memory. Let me give you a quick history lesson. Our ancestors brought them here from

Europe and turned them into slaves. Whatever woman a man wanted, he brought her into his house, so he could rape her at his leisure. Whenever he grew tired of her, he sent her into the fields to pick cotton. The men worked countless hours in the fields. If they couldn't handle it, they were hanged. It was because of their pale skin, devilish-colored eyes, and straight hair."

Mr. Carver imagined the abuses those people suffered. "Do you think that's fair? What if they did that to us? I don't think we would've liked it."

The shocked guests were unable to reply, but Judge Turner said, "I don't agree with your plan, and I know a lot of people here feel the same way. Thanks for the invitation, but we'll be leaving." He turned to his wife. "Get the kids. Let's go."

Other guests began moving toward the door.

"So you want to leave?" Mr. Carver asked. "You can get out!"

Seeing Mr. Fiorini leaving, he said, "Not you, Mr. Fiorini. This has really upset me."

"I'd better go. I caused enough trouble already." Shaking Mr. Carver's hand, he said good-bye.

Mr. Carver was so disappointed, he went to his room. Claudia knew he was upset, so she remained downstairs and said good-bye to the guests, offering her apologies.

After giving her husband a couple of hours to cool off, she went upstairs and walked into their bedroom. "Are you all right, Honey?"

"Yeah, but I expected a different outcome."

"I know. What do you want to do?"

"I did what you said. I prayed about it and read the Bible. It says to love they neighbor as thyself. I know God meant for us to love each other, 'cause the Bible doesn't specify color or whether someone is rich or poor. If you read the Declaration of Independence, it has the words, *All men are created equal.* Why would they write it like that if they didn't mean it? It doesn't make sense.

"Come Monday, I'll do whatever it takes to get on the ballot for the Governor's race."

"You're absolutely right," she said. "It doesn't make any sense. I support you one hundred percent."

"Thank you, Honey," he said gratefully. "I love you so much."

"I love you, too. Let's get some rest. It's been another long day."

Just like the previous night, Mr. Carver started thrashing and talking in his sleep. He began screaming, shouting, "Let me go! No, no, no! Let me go!"

When he awoke, he wasn't in bed with his wife. He was in front of two White policemen in a jail cell.

"What am I doing here?" he asked. "What are y'all doing to me."

"You must've been having a good dream, 'cause we've been trying to wake you for a while. Boy, you're goin' to hang for trying to steal that horse."

"No! I wasn't stealing! That horse is mine. I'm one of the richest men in the South. Please let me go. This is a mistake! My name is Nathaniel Carver, but everyone calls me Mr. Carver."

The officers looked at each other and started laughing.

"This dumb nigger done lost his mind when he bumped his head," one said.

"No!" he shouted. "My name's Mr. Carver!"

"Come on, Mr. Carver. They're waiting for you outside."

The two men laughed again.

They took him outside the courthouse to be publicly hanged for stealing. As he walked between them, he realized it was all a dream.

The officers walked him up the platform, tied his hands behind his back, and placed a rope around his neck. He thought how real the dream had been, only to turn into a nightmare.

The officer opened the trapdoor, and a moment later, he hung there dead, along with his dream of changing the world.

CHAPTER 8

THE LITTLE RAPPER

James Moore

Once upon a time there was a little girl named Katie, who loved rap music. All she ever thought about was being a rap singer. Day in, day out, Katie rapped. She listened to Ice-T, LL Cool J, McHammer, and DJ Quick, but her favorite was Chris Brown.

Her parents enjoyed the way she moved and hip hopped to the music she listened to.

"One day," she told her mom, "I'm going to write the lyrics to my very own rap song."

She sat down in her room and wrote the lyrics to a song called *The Katie Rap.* When she finished, she left her room and went to her mom. "Will you listen to the lyrics I wrote?"

Katie started singing and dancing for her mom. When she finished, her mother hugged her and said, "That was fantastic, Katie. I love your new song.

The following day, Katie took her lyrics to school for Show and Tell. She sang and danced her song to her class, and her classmates loved it.

Katie didn't realize that one of the students in class who also played and sang music had her dad, Mr. O'Malley, with her that day. He heard Katie's song and asked if she'd sing and dance for him at his music studio.

"If it's OK with my mom, it's OK with me," she replied. "Let me ask her first."

"I'll ask her for you if you want me to," the man said. "She can bring you to my music studio, and you can sing your rap lyrics for me there."

Katie went home and asked her mom, who said it was OK. Katie was excited all week, waiting for Saturday to arrive, so she could visit a real live recording studio.

At ten o'clock that Saturday morning, Mr. O'Malley met Katie and her mom at the studio door.

"My God, this place is fantastic!" Katie said, looking at the sound equipment, microphones, drums, guitars, an organ, a turntable, the mixing board, boom mikes, lights, and the sound room.

She gasped in delight, while Mr. O'Mally smiled.

"Katie, step into the studio for a sound take," he said. "You should do a practice run, so we can adjust the equipment to your voice."

She walked into the studio and froze. "I can't do this. I'm scared."

"Just pretend you're in class at school, doing this for Show and Tell day."

Katie shut her eyes for a second and said, "OK. I'm ready." She started singing and dancing like at school.

After the sound check, Mr. O'Mally said, "We're ready to record you now."

Katie didn't know that Chris Brown, the famous rapper, was in town for a benefit to help the local food bank. As she did her lyrics a second time, Chris walked in and told his band to add music to her song.

"Let's gangsta together, Little One," he told Katie.

Chris Brown, his band, and Katie recorded *The Katie Rap.*

That night, Katie prayed on her knees beside her bed. "Thank You, God, for Mr. O'Mally, my Show and Tell class, and the great Chris Brown."

The Katie Rap became number one on the hip hop and rap charts. Katie stayed in school, helping other kids fulfill their dreams of being stars. Katie gave concerts in her town to help the homeless, the poor, and those in need. The money she raised helped many people, and Katie was loved by all.

This can happen to anyone who believes in him- or herself. Never say you can't do something. Always think positively. Never quit. Finish everything you start. Maybe someday you can be a rap star, a country singer, a movie star, or even become president.

We all make our own future. We need to stay in school, get an education, take up music or dance—whatever our dream is—and go for it. We are the future generation.

CHAPTER 9

A LIFE HALF-REMEMBERED

Theresà Easson

CHAPTER ONE

On a candleholder I once read the words, *Memories: We do not remember days, we remember moments.* I've thought about those words, and it's true that we remember only moments.

At the moment, these words are being taken down by my daughter, because I'm unable to control a pen or anything. It's not through being lazy but ill health. I have time to think and remember.

Most memories I don't wish to remember. Others aren't so bad. Time drags when one is forced to stay in bed all the time. It's a pity my body doesn't work, but my mind does. Which is worse, the mind or the body not working? I wish at times my mind didn't think so much of the past, but there's little in the future to think about

What are my first memories? Time doesn't dull them. They aren't good ones. I remember being in the pram, hidden with the hood up and my bonnet pulled down. I didn't understand it, because it wasn't raining. The sun was shining. The woman pushing the pram was my mother, so why keep me hidden?

Apparently, as I learned later in life, I was ugly due to the forceps used to help with my birth. My face became badly scarred.

The doctor was out drinking that night and couldn't keep the forceps straight.

All the time I grew up, I was kept out of the way. To make matters worse, my hair was cut by placing a pudding basin on my head and trimming around it. As a child, I was short and fat. With my hair cut that way and a scarred face, I wasn't a pleasant sight. I understand why my mother wasn't happy with my appearance.

She had a lovely baby boy when I was four-years old, one she could be proud of. He was fair-headed with a bonny, perfect face, not like me. Mother showed him off to the world, feeling proud and happy, while hiding me away.

Everyone cooed over him, and I hated him. One day, I thought if I got rid of my brother, everything would be fine. I was only four, so I hope others will make allowances.

He was in the garden in his pram. I pushed the pram over the grass to the gate, opened it, and moved onto the pavement. The pram began rolling downhill.

I don't remember who saved him, but I got into dreadful trouble. I was never allowed to be alone with him after that. It was awful being watched all the time, never trusted again. Life went on for a few years that way. It's hard to remember how long.

My mind flits from one moment to the next. Is it trying to avoid some of the worst things that happened to me, or should I think of funny times?

I was raised in a French convent school in the West Country, where I went after prep school. The other girls bullied me a lot for my appearance, and my life was grim. Children can be very cruel. Life in the convent was horrid. The nuns were kind, and they never saw what the other girls said or did.

I got up one morning and for some reason, I was in a different mood. I found myself at the top of the stairs leading down to the breakfast hall. The ringleader walked past, smirking as usual, and I saw red. I punched her face. She was too surprised to call out.

Overbalancing, she fell down the stairs. Nuns ran in from all directions. Thankfully, the only hurt was to the girl's pride. She damaged a front tooth, which meant a lot of dental work at my father's expense. He wasn't happy about that.

The worst thing was sitting in the entrance hall with my luggage, waiting for my father. I received terrible stares from the nuns and the other girls. Some just giggled. I felt terrible, because no one bothered to speak to me and ask why I did it.

I sat there for hours until my father arrived. He didn't acknowledge me or look at me. Instead, he walked straight into Mother Superior's office and remained inside for a long time. I feared the worst.

He paid compensation to the girl and agreed to cover her dental expenses, and I was allowed to stay. I always wondered if he paid the convent something just to keep me. The only good thing to come out of that incident was that the other girls never picked on me again.

I learned piano and passed my music exams. I loved dancing. We were allowed to do the *Dance of the Seven Veils*, which was fun. I was good enough at tennis to represent my school.

I had fun with the nuns and some of the other girls and even made friends after the incident. Before I left the convent to start life as an adult, Mother Superior pointed out that I had a lot going for me. I was accomplished at sports and at reading music and playing the piano. My painting and drawing were at a high standard. With my sewing and embroidery skills, this should stand me in good stead in life. My singing voice was always in demand, especially because I knew four languages. I learned Latin at the convent as one should to become fit for marriage and society. Mother Superior added that my prospects were excellent, and I should go far in life.

If only that were true. The life I hoped for never materialized.

Those days are long gone, and life is very different. I stare out a window most of the time. The view is lovely. In Scotland's countryside I see deer roaming the hills. I hear the nearby river, which is a true river, not a burn.

It's a lovely day. The sun is out, and I hear birds singing, sounding out their spring song. I'm lucky not to be placed in a nursing home, as some children do to their parents when they become old or infirm, becoming a burden and are no longer useful. It's nice to be in my own home.

I still have some control over my life, so in a way, I'm contented, though I regret the choices I made. If only we could go back and start over again. I would have liked to have done things differently. I only hope that what I expect of my daughter isn't too much for her.

I have a bad habit of telling her, "If only I had my legs. I'd do this for myself!" She does as asked every time. I knew what I was doing, of course. It was emotional blackmail.

I feel ashamed for asking her to do my bidding all the time. She has no time for herself. How could she? I've been so unfeeling. None of my other children did anything to assist her physically or financially. My son gave her two half-days off in ten years. My daughter cares for me seven days a week with no holidays or time off. The government doesn't pay a caregiver much, so she has no treats, just bills.

Again, my mind is wandering to the day I married for the first time. Although my face was scarred, the scars faded over time, and, with makeup, they didn't look that bad. It was odd that I was asked to model hats and go into films.

I grew to be six-feet tall and very slender. I took a film test in Earls Court many years ago when I was eighteen. They said the scars were no problem, because they had makeup artists.

I was thrilled, but my parents objected. It was a different life then. They did the same thing later. I had a mezzo-soprano voice, unusual for an Englishwoman. Welsh women are more likely to have such a voice.

Again, my family said no to the chance for me to sing, because it wasn't suitable for a young lady. I was supposed to make a proper marriage to enhance my family's position. I was well-educated so I could fit into society.

I married, but it wasn't happy. Was I in love? Who knows? I had never received affection from anyone, so the first person who acted warm toward me was the one I married. I thought that was love, but I learned different. If I'd been raised with love in my home, I might have been wiser.

While I was trapped in that awful marriage, I met a lovely man who wished to marry me, but once again, my parents said, "No." In the end, my marriage failed miserably. We divorced while I was carrying my first child, a girl. My husband refused to recognize the child as his. That was in the days when there were no benefits for a woman in such a situation. I was left without any help from family.

I was frightened, not knowing where to turn for help. I had no qualifications to obtain work. I wanted to be an architect like my father. If they had allowed it, I would have been in a better position to care for my child and myself. Maybe I would have understood life better, too, and not made so many mistakes along the way.

I walked the streets, looking for a home, and finally found rooms. It was different from what I grew up with. There were no servants to do all that was needed to run a household—no chauffeur-driven cars, no gardeners, no maids to wait on me. I loved the servants, who were always kind to me and looked after me. When I was small, they took me into the kitchen and spoiled me with home-baked biscuits and cakes. Above all, they spoke to me as if I mattered.

Living on my own, I found life daunting. I was frightened. My father shut the door on me, so there would be no help from him or any member of our extended family. Everyone shunned me. It was a desperate feeling to be so alone and frightened in life. I cried myself to sleep for hours each night, but I felt no better.

I stood in that room alone with my child, wondering what to do. I had a beautiful little girl to care for. Life went on. I always worried about money or its lack. As long as I could care for my child, though, life would be fine—or so I told myself.

After a time, I met a chap who came from South Africa, a game warden who said he would care for me and my child. I thought my life finally changed for the better. Maybe I could return to the family fold once I was married again without any stigma attached to me or my child.

Life doesn't work out so easily. Why was I stupid enough to believe all the lies? Was I that blind? The chap seemed decent and said all the right things. He said he loved me. We were to marry and go to South Africa. He would take care of me and my daughter and raise her as his own.

My life had finally taken a turn for the better, and I was happy, but.... There is always a *but*.

He was already married, something I learned by accident. When I discovered this fact, I was already pregnant with my second child. The man ran back to his mother and his wife and hid behind them. When I tried to see him, I saw only his mother and wife, who refused to let me see him. I tried to forget the horrid words they called me, while the man hid upstairs. Devastated and dazed, I couldn't think what to do next. I felt numb and sick.

The rooms where I stayed would be too small for me with two children. They were only a year different in age. It was hard enough feeding one child, and I suddenly faced the prospect of two babies to feed and clothe. There were no charity shops or secondhand clothing stores.

The landlord and landlady said I had to leave straightaway. They didn't want their house gaining a reputation for allowing whores. That was the first time that word was used against me, though it wasn't the last. I didn't see myself as a whore. I fell in love with a man, and we had a love child.

CHAPTER TWO

I searched everywhere for a place to stay. I finally found something in a village fifty miles away, not a very good place, but at least it had a roof. It was difficult to clean and make it seem a better place to live. The neighbors refused to speak to me and stared, whispering behind my back.

My second child was born there. My grandmother came to stay with me for a home birth. She was the only one who helped. My mother was too busy, her usual excuse. By that time, my father divorced her for a slimmer, younger woman. The usual reasons made it even harder for her to accept her situation. She had to work, because she frittered away all the money from the divorce settlement.

No one but my dear grandmother would speak to me, and I thanked God she was in my life. My stepmother was awful to me, but my brother was accepted and would fit in as her child, whereas I couldn't fit it even before I was in trouble.

With my grandmother's help, I gave birth to a beautiful girl. There was no district nurse in attendance, though someone arrived immediately after the birth to cut the cord and make sure the baby and I were well. Strangers looked at my girls and told me how lucky I was to have two such beautiful children.

I was proud of them, but I wished I could do more for them. All I had was love. It was difficult for them to be born illegitimate. Life is different now, and those things don't seem to matter as much. Many young people have relationships with different partners, producing offspring, and no one seems to care. It's almost normal for a woman to have children from different fathers.

When my dear grandmother went home, life seemed much worse. I was alone again, which I found terrifying. I tried not to pass on those dreadful feelings to my children and gave them only contentment. Everything a person feels in such situations seems to bubble up to the surface. I never thought of ending my life, though I wondered if my children would have been better off adopted.

My father always said, "Put them in a home, then you can return to the fold." How could I do that when I gave birth to them? I wanted my children. Was I being obtuse? Would they have been better off?

They were mine. I had nothing else in life to call my own. When my eldest was twelve, an older couple offered to adopt her. They were in a position to give her all that I couldn't. They had money. She would have a pony, a good school, and all the clothes she desired. Later in life, I learned she would have loved that and blamed me for not letting her go, but I couldn't do it. Was I being selfish?

I must stop thinking now, as my daughter has arrived to prepare me for the day. It's hard work. She has to wash me, which means turning me over, then she must wash the sheets. She always dresses my long hair, putting it up, as I can no longer do. Am I letting her do too much for me? Am I too demanding?

I suppose I must be. It's the first time I've thought about that. I hate remembering all the mistakes I've made and how hard her life must be.

CHAPTER THREE

Today is a new day. I must stop thinking of the past. I wonder why we do that. It's as if we're punishing ourselves. When it's miserable and wet outside, our thoughts travel back in time. That was a time I wish I could forget, but it happened, and I can't hide from it.

I lived in a dreadful hovel with only a few scraps of food to eat each day, trying to eke out a living. I never had extra clothing or shoes, just one set, making it difficult to wash and dry when I had nothing else to put on. I won't mention my underwear. I felt desolate, and I thought life couldn't get any worse.

Again, life sent surprises—some desperate ones.

One morning I woke and saw to the children as usual. I fed and washed my baby girls and washed their little clothes. I bought a few balls of wool and knitted their bonnets, jackets, and booties, although I had to teach myself how to knit.

As least I could hand down the garments as the eldest grew. I clothed my second daughter more easily than the first. I was in my little kitchen, which contained a sink with a cold-water tap—no hot water—a tiny cooker, and a tiny table with one old chair.

My children were outside in the garden when a neighbor came quietly up behind me, grabbed me, and held me down. I was strong in those days, but I didn't have the strength to fight him off, and I was weakened by lack of food. He raped me, and I couldn't do anything about it.

Dear God, I thought, *how much more of this life must I endure?*

The only thing my assailant said when he finished was, "I've always wanted to do that." He walked away.

When I told his sisters about it, they said I deserved it and called me a whore. There was no point going to the police. They would do nothing. I was a single mother with two children.

Life grew worse. I couldn't walk down the street without hearing catcalls or stones being thrown at me. I was worried the stones would hit one of my girls. It was dreadful for the little ones to witness the hatred of adults.

Once again, I had to seek new accommodation. Where should I start? I had no transport and could only afford one newspaper a week to look for a rental. I took country buses to see if other villages might have accommodation.

It took a fortnight, but I finally found some rooms, though they weren't very auspicious. A beggar has little choice. One hovel was like another.

Then I discovered I was pregnant again. Soon, I would have three children to look after. Why was all this happening to me? It wasn't my fault. I could be blamed for the first time, but not the second or third.

Again, I implored my grandmother to come for the birth. I received threats from others to take my two girls away. I couldn't bear to think about it. My dear grandmother came to my rescue and stayed with me for the birth of my third child.

Giving birth to a bouncing boy, I was very happy. I assumed he would protect me once he grew up. He was my golden-haired, blue-eyed boy, so I would no longer have to worry.

I was wrong. It turned out to be my youngest daughter who always cared for me. As my girls grew up, I often said, "I wish I had boys, not girls." Later, I wondered how a mother could say that to her children. It was cruel and hurtful. Hadn't I been hurt enough to know better? Did my youngest look after me out of guilt or gratitude? I hope she loves me.

Did I make her feel guilty, because I took care of my children and refused to place them in an orphanage for unwanted children? I suffered hardships but felt it was my duty to keep my family together.

My mind is racing again, unable to stop. I remember days of going without food and sucking on a leather belt. That didn't help much, though it kept my mind off food for a while. I heard somewhere that's what people did when they were starving.

More often than not, I didn't have a fire to keep us warm, and I worried my children might catch colds. I kept them in bed cuddled up with me for warmth with a few old bits of blankets.

It broke my heart. My children didn't deserve such a life. They were innocent, so why were they being punished for something they didn't do? I kept wondering if I should have put them up for adoption. Was I making them suffer? I could have changed their circumstances very easily if I wanted. Having been unwanted as a child, I didn't want my children to experience that.

I have searched my soul over this issue many times until I'm no longer sure of anything. I must stop beating myself up over it.

CHAPTER FOUR

Another day dawned like all the others. Nothing made any difference in my life except for occasional doctor visits. I heard classical music coming from a radio. I have always loved classical music and remember singing arias as I tidied up my small home. That was my only escape from my worries. Anyone in such a situation will understand. No one should live in such a hellhole.

I eventually met the chap next door. I never spoke to anyone in town except the shopkeeper. One day, however, my eldest daughter told our neighbour how hungry she was. He was divorced and living alone.

He offered to have me move in with him and bring the children. It wasn't my first choice, but I did. I once met a coal merchant who had five children to care for after his wife left him. He offered to take me and my three children in. I feared he would put my children last. Was refusing him a mistake on my part? He had money, so I'd never have to worry about finances again. That would have been a relief. He said we could have a child together, too, but I didn't want the family to become so large that I couldn't cope.

My father would have been happy with such an arrangement. The man had his own business, making him more acceptable. It wouldn't have mattered to my father if the marriage was happy, as long as I married someone with money.

In the end, I refused him.

My neighbour, however, had one son from his first marriage, but the boy was in his mid-twenties and left home years earlier. I thought that was a safer bet for my children. The question of love never entered my mind. It would be a marriage of convenience for us both.

I would take care of the house and chores, as well as helping with paperwork. He would work and bring home the money. It wasn't the best basis for a relationship. He was twenty-four-years older, born in 1898. We faced many differences socially and in how we were raised. He loved his mother and hated his father, because the man was a drunkard and beat his wife. His father owned his own farm, but my neighbour moved out once his mother died. His father remarried and burned down the house one night while drunk.

He never saw his father again after leaving home. He rarely mentioned him or his early life. He had a brother and two sisters, but he never communicated with them.

I decided to move in with my neighbour. It was difficult, because he was a stranger to me. I imagine it was the same for him. Life continued, still with very little money, because he didn't make much. With five of us, our budget was tight, but we scraped along. When I think back on it, it seems incredible that one would 0fall into a relationship like that with a virtual stranger. Even with an arranged marriage, I would have known the man better.

We managed a life that seemed full of work and worry for both of us. I don't know if he ever had any regrets. I certainly did. I never asked. Now that I'm older, I wish I knew the answer. It's funny how things come to a person as she ages. When I was young, I didn't have the time or inclination to ask.

I hope he was happy, but I don't see how. He always worked long, hard hours. He came home only to eat and sleep, with hardly a day off. Even at Christmas and Easter, he volunteered to work. The only thing he liked was his pipe, which seemed to make him content. He sat down in the evening, smoking his honey-dew tobacco, and it kept him in a good mood.

He enlisted in the First World War just before his sixteenth birthday. They didn't care about ages back then. He was badly wounded and left to die, because the doctors thought nothing could be done for him. Shrapnel in the back of his neck gave him terrible headaches. When he got in a bad temper, all of us knew to stay away. If the children did anything wrong or upset him, he would go after them, and I had to stand in his way. I took the beatings for them, refusing to let him lay a hand on any of them.

My son annoyed him, taking his tools without asking, then losing them or leaving them in the grass to become rusty. My eldest girl was finicky about food, which also angered him. I couldn't risk letting him strike them, because I didn't know how far he would go.

I lost count of how many times he pressed a knife against my throat, or tried to push me from the upstairs windows. What else could I have done? The police would never take action in a domestic dispute. In their eyes, he had the right to chastise his wife and children.

Though life was bad at times, I also found a few occasions to laugh. The events weren't that funny, but I saw the funny side, anyway.

It's odd what remains in my mind, when at other times, I try to forget.

CHAPTER FIVE

One lovely day, the sun was out, warming the air. My second child decided to go fishing in the pig pond. She climbed the small wall, slipped into the mud, and went down. My son tried to hold her up, while my youngest ran for me.

She was covered from head to toe in pig muddy water. All we had for bathing was a small, galvanized outside tub. It took a long time to heat enough water and keep her still so I could wash her, then her clothes. I lost the entire morning.

Another time, I slipped out of the house for half an hour to visit a neighbour. My eldest sat on a kitchen chair, and my second eldest decided to wash her hair. It wouldn't have been so bad if she used water, but for some reason, she opened a tin of syrup. To make matters worse, she rubbed a packet of tea in her hair.

It was a terrible mess. It sounds funny now, but we couldn't afford to waste those items.

My son did a dreadful thing one day. He and his pals hid behind a short wall and told my youngest girl to put a stick down a hole. Out came three wasps. When they told her to do it again, the whole nest attacked. I heard her screaming and ran after her.

She was so badly stung, she couldn't stand. She was dizzy with the poison. I could barely see her under the wasps. Thank God none entered her mouth, or she would have died.

If I told her father, he would have strapped my son for pulling such a prank. It took her years to get over it, and I felt guilty. I never yelled at my children, especially my darling son. In my eyes, he could do no wrong.

He liked to abuse my youngest girl. She was so innocent, I hoped she never understood what was happening. She was only four at the time. My eldest daughter caught him abusing her and came directly to me. I brought the two children to me and told my beloved boy, "Never do this again."

I later learned he abused her for many more years. I asked her about it years later to see if he stopped. She admitted he hadn't stopped, but she didn't say anything in case her father found out, because he would beat me for it.

That's why I never understood why she nursed me for so many years. I let her down, and I always put my son first, finding excuses for him. I even had the cheek to ask her, when I finally leave this world, to look after him.

How could I do such a thing? Once he hit her in the head so hard, he fractured her skull, but I begged her not to go to the hospital, because my son would end up in trouble. She suffered pain for many months and years but still nursed me.

How could I do that to her? She was the only one of my girls who cared enough to bother with me. I've heard other people say their sons looked after them.

I have to stop thinking. It's too hard to remember how uncaring I was when I let such things happen. Was I so blind about my son that I actually thought he would look after me? He always lived his life the way he wanted without a care for anyone else.

I can't stop myself from thinking. I remember all the injuries my daughter suffered while caring for me. Her shoulder was partially dislocated, she was burned on the face and arms, and she lost a lot of hair around her face. She was burned badly enough that flesh came off her nose when she blew it. The second time she was burned, it affected her legs and toes. She had first- second-and third-degree burns. She was supposed to put up her legs and stay off her feet

She drove me to my son's house 200 miles away, hoping he would stay home to care for me, but he went to work as usual, taking his sister to the hospital only at night to have her bandages changed. She was left to care for me again without any help.

Why didn't I see that? Was I blind to have put such faith in him? It was because of the way other men treated me all my life. My daughter never reproached me once for the way her brother treated her. She just accepted it.

I blame myself for what happened to her, but I can't change the past. Did I really do all I could for my children? I went without food and clothing, but I tried to make up for our lack with all the love I could give. Was it enough?

I have to stop thinking now. It's too hard to bear all these thoughts. Having to make love to someone I didn't love was like being a prostitute. I didn't blame him for his bad temper. That came from his wounds in the war. I hated the violence my children saw while growing up.

Is that why my son still thinks it's all right to hit women? He always had a violent streak, fighting with younger boys. He chased a boy into his own house and broke furniture, trying to hit him, and I did nothing about it. Was that how he learned to be violent? He even hit my girls when they were in their teens, and I still did nothing.

I realize I should have been firmer with him and not let him get away with so much. I used to tell my youngest daughter to do whatever my son said, because he would look after her. I instilled this in her from an early age. If I hadn't said that, perhaps she wouldn't have been abused. The fact that she never reproached me for her life makes me feel even worse. It seemed living the life I had left me too engrossed in survival to pay attention to other things.

My mind jumps from one memory to another. I recall the day my youngest was born. It was a hot July day, a real scorcher, a very uncomfortable time to be pregnant.

I didn't want any more children. For me, three was enough. Everyone says their babies are beautiful, but mine really were. They looked six-months old at birth. Even the district nurses wondered how they emerged without wrinkles and red skin, especially with my diet. I was slightly disappointed when I had my third girl, but, on reflection, what would I have done with another boy? I might have made the same mistakes I did with the first.

CHAPTER SIX

Different memories run through my mind, good and bad. My daughter walked miles pushing my wheelchair, so I could be in the fresh air and see different things. She saved money to learn how to drive. I never knew why she took a heavy-goods vehicle license class one, as it was called. Perhaps it was because her brother had a class three, and she wanted to have a higher class.

We bought an old ambulance, and we traveled all over. I had a bed in the back. We covered most of the counties in England, toured Scotland, and managed to see Wales, too. It was hard work for my daughter. We had great times exploring the British Isles, seeing places most people never saw. The last twenty years of my life were good, though we had the usual worries. It would have been a lot worse without someone to care for me. I was fortunate to have one child who did.

My happiest time in life was when I was thirteen. I had a bicycle, which for me represented freedom. I cycled all over the South Downs. It was glorious. I met some gentlemen of the road, who others would call tramps. They were interesting, and I learned about their lives and how they became travelers. They talked to me as if I mattered. The sense of freedom was so uplifting, I spent hours away from home, content on my bicycle.

The sandwiches I brought with me were made of bread and condensed, sweetened milk. They were lovely, sticky and sweet, a lunch from heaven. Those are the days I remember most. I suppress other memories and try to remember the good times.

I wonder if it's almost my time to depart this life. I feel apprehensive, because I have so much to ask forgiveness for. I know we judge ourselves on the other side, but it's harder to judge yourself than for others to judge us. I dread finding out all the hurt I caused. How could I make up for that?

I'm so tired of lying in bed, thinking back over my life. It's not a life to be proud of. I hope I brought some happiness into the lives of people I knew, especially my children. I hope when I depart this earth, it'll be while I sleep. Time is short for me. I've been seeing my father, ready to take me home, which shows me that he, at least, loved me.

I feel dreadful that my daughter will be left alone, without a husband or children. What will happen to her?

It's too late now. My father beckons. My daughter knows my time is near, but I don't think she knows how quickly I will leave her. It's hard to say good-bye to those you love, but we all must do it someday.

I'll sleep now, and say, "Good-bye and God bless."

CHAPTER 10

THE RED RADIO FLYER WAGON

Bob Bernotus

In the 1950s, my dad worked hard at the steel mill all week, trying to scrape together enough to raise ten kids and keep us all in Catholic school. Every night during the week, he came home from work, exhausted, and fell into a chair to listen to the radio, but Friday night was his night for time with his friends.

Along about eight o'clock on Friday night, after the six of us kids who were still left at home finished eating, Mom would say, "It's time to go get your dad, Bobby."

Out the door I'd go, down the railroad tracks, turn right and down two blocks, to find my dad at the tavern, having shots and beers. Every time he saw me, his face split open into a grin. "Hey, Bobbyo. What you doin' Kiddo?"

"Your supper's ready, Dad."

I steadied his steps as we walked back home to our little rented home.

Every cent had to be accounted for in our poor home, including what Dad spent for his shots and beers on Friday night. We could hardly afford them, but Mom considered them reward for all his hard work.

It became painfully aware just how scarce money was when those nuns used to say, in front of a schoolroom full of kids, "Bernotus!

Your parents haven't sent your quarter for this month's tuition. Do you have it?"

Under the staring glares of all the other students, I'd just shake my head and look down, wanting to be anywhere but in that classroom.

One Friday night, I found Dad sitting on the bar stool next to another mill worker, striking up some kind of a deal. "Three dollars," Dad said, "and not a cent more."

"Six," his fellow mill worker, Frank, said. "You know how much they cost new?"

"It ain't new, though," Dad said. "It's been beat up by three of your kids. Four dollars. And that's final."

"Five," Frank said. "Five bucks and it's yours. And you might wanna throw in a shot and a beer."

Dad pulled out six wrinkled hard-earned singles, gave one to the bartender for "another round," and the rest he gave to Frank, who scooted out the front door and came back in pulling a red Radio Flyer wagon behind him.

"Is that for us?" I asked Dad.

"It sure is, Bobbyo," said Dad. He emptied his shot, slugged back his beer, and climbed down off of his bar stool. "Let's go home."

"But what will Mom say?"

"Ah, she'll love it, Kiddo. You'll see." Dad clapped his arm around my shoulder, and we started off down the street.

With each revolution, one of the wheels screamed, "Shreeee...." There we were, a tall beanpole man, steadied by a short eight year old, pulling along a squeaky wagon.

Mom was waiting with his warmed-up supper when we got home. She eyed the wagon suspiciously. "Where'd that come from?"

"It was a bargain," Dad said.

"What we need that for?"

"You'll see tomorrow. I'm takin' the kids to the beach!"

Mom just stood on tiptoe, kissed his cheek, and hustled his warmed-up beans and ham from the oven, a small smile hiding on her face.

Every Saturday after that, us kids, three boys and three girls, could hardly stay in bed on Saturday mornings, even though we knew it was the only day of the week Dad could sleep late. We tried to be quiet for him, but the weekly trip to the beach was just too wonderful.

The wagon wouldn't hold all of us, so we started out with the three girls riding and the three boys walking. It took about 45 minutes to get to Rainbow Beach on Lake Michigan. Halfway there, it was time for the girls to get out and let the boys ride the rest of the way.

All the way there, the wheel "shreee, shreee, shreeed," despite the fact that Dad had oiled it with everything he could think of. The night I first saw the Radio Flyer in that saloon, I thought it was the most-beautiful chariot I would ever see. In the sunlight, though, it was a bit battered and scratched, but we sure loved it.

Dad toted along a quart of Miester Brau Beer for himself and lemonade and bologna sandwiches on Wonder Bread with mustard, wrapped in waxed paper, for us kids. When we got to the beach, we ate in shifts. The girls ate first.

They had to wait a half an hour before they could go in the water, so they wouldn't get cramps. While they were splashing around with Dad, us boys ate our sandwiches, so by the time it was our turn in the water, we were safe from the dreaded deadly cramps.

By the time we ate, the lemonade was warm and watery, the bologna sandwiches were hot, and somehow beach sand found its way into the sandwiches. Each mouthful was hot, mustardy, and gritty, but we loved every bite.

Dad rubbed us down with baby oil mixed with iodine, to keep us from burning. We built sand castles, buried each other in the sand, and jumped off Dad's broad shoulders into the water.

After a few hours at the beach, it was time to go home, the boys riding first, and halfway there the girls took their turn, the wagon wheel screaming, and all of us laughing. We arrived home wet, burned, exhausted, and happy.

One day Mom heard that wagon wheel screaming as I hauled coal from the garage to the house. She ran into the house and came back out carrying the aluminum container that held bacon grease next to our stove. She doused that wheel axel with bacon grease, and it never squealed again.

Over the years, and its many, many trips to the beach, after being exposed to water, sand, and kids, the wagon became pretty beat-up. It peeled like we did when we sunburned. I kept after it with sandpaper and paintbrush, trying to keep it going for as long as we needed it. Eventually, the words, "Radio Flyer" were obscured with red paint.

Mom grew up in an orphanage. She was fifteen when she met Dad, at a dance the orphanage gave to try to encourage romance and marriage between the boys in town and the orphan girls. He was nineteen, and they soon married and started their family. She was five feet two inches, Irish, and as spherical as a human being could be. He was six feet three, Polish, handsome, and lanky.

Their union lasted for 53 years. I was raising my own family of three girls and a boy in a big two-story house, when I bought the coach house out in front, to give my parents a place to stay, so I could see after them as they aged. The day they moved in, here came Dad, hauling folded clothes in that old red Radio Flyer.

After a horrible bout with cancer that lasted a year, my mother died. Their whole lives had been so entwined with each other Dad just didn't seem to know how to function without her.

I stopped in to see him every night on my way home from work. One day, he said, "Your mother came to see me, Bobbyo."

"No, now Dad, you know Ma's been gone for months now."

"But she did. She was here."

I didn't know what to say. He must have sensed my discomfort, because then he said, "Why don't you come over after you eat? Well have a shot and a beer. What about it, huh?"

"Sure, Dad. A shot and a beer. Sounds good."

The request was so unusual, I should have sensed something was wrong.

Late that night, after supper, after the shot and the beer with Dad, when I was sound asleep back in my own bed in the big house, I suddenly heard the sound of that old wagon wheel, going "Shreeee," in my head. I sat up bed, instantly awake. My mouth was filled with the taste of warm lemonade and hot bologna sandwiches on Wonder Bread with mustard, gritty with sand.

I pulled on my pants and ran out the back door to the front house. I pushed and pushed on the door to Dad's house, but something was blocking it. I finally got in the door and found Dad sprawled on the floor, in front of the door.

He had a heart attack. He was trying to go out the back door, to come to me for help, when he died. I called the ambulance, then got down on the floor and cradled him in my arms as I waited for them to come.

When I looked down at him, though, I didn't see the old man, his porcelain skin tinged with blue, sprawled lifelessly on the floor. Instead, I saw him young, handsome, tall, and lanky, filled with laughter and love, hauling his kids to Rainbow Beach in that wonderful old red Radio Flyer.

CHAPTER 11

UNDERCLASSED

Oz Greek

When writing, draw from your own personal experiences. A fight broke out in the city courtyard. Many people got involved looking for the one who started the trouble. A kid, brought to trial in front of the entire kingdom, was accused of falsehood and sabotage. People became enraged, pointing fingers at him. How many people deal with life using complete professionalism? It rarely happens.

That was where the story began, based on factual events.

The elders learned that the city played head-hunting games to seek competitive advantage in a search for treasure maps. Would the elders become involved? Did those maps really exist? Who was the kid, and what did he do to bring such attention to himself?

People returned to their daily routines, but something felt different to the kid. He decided to move on and not cause any trouble. Though he listened to conversation around him, he didn't react to it.

First things first: Know what you're talking about and who you're dealing with. People exist in different places in their lives and need any advantage they can muster to succeed. Some return to school, while others try opening businesses. People always hope that nurturing the right kind of relationships with genuine intentions is good enough, but that's not always the case.

What seems like being exiled by society and receiving constant cold-shoulder treatments is actually a character-development exercise and indifference. The kid intermingled with his peers in an attempt to move on. Those who cut him out also plotted against him, searching for the many treasure maps and blueprints people talked about. Who would win in a battle of wits for prestige and dominance among the elders and people of the kingdom?

The elders knew many stories about hidden keys and maps revealing secrets, with blueprints leading to treasures only few attained. While the world's brightest sought privacy, society sought community and wondered why some people wanted seclusion. What were they hiding or avoiding talking about with their peers? Some said, "Absolutely nothing."

A second thing to remember is to get rid of arguments against people. Even if those arguments are true, they'll only make a person seem angry and resentful, and that holds back success.

At a young age, the kid was given a book of secrets. The more he read the book, the more he learned about people and life. The book gave an in-depth perspective about life's generalities and mysteries. It also held blueprints to treasure maps and secret locations.

Hidden with the book the kid's father gave him was a key and a map blueprint. The blueprint disclosed locations that had to be excavated to unearth clues to the map's mysteries. The map was passed from generation to generation as a gift within the family. The kid wanted to avoid bringing attention to himself, hoping he could decode the map with as little help as possible.

He wanted to gift his family with treasure and continue the tradition. Inscribed on the key were numbers to a safe. He remembered an old safe his father showed him hidden in an old house where they once lived.

A third thing to remember is that people don't have to compromise what they are to please others. One never earns other people's respect if he has no principles of his own. People should remain true to themselves and do whatever they can to help others.

The kid felt that people in the city had, for years, talked about what they wanted to get their hands on, and he didn't want them finding out what he was up to. He couldn't shake the awkward feeling he got when he met others. He knew he wasn't innocent, but he wasn't what people believed, either.

While everyone tried to involve the kid in activities, all he wanted was to get away. He studied all he could in his free time, hoping to learn what the others were talking about. When would he have to face the unknown, and how would he deal with the aftermath? It seemed like people expected to catch him being vulnerable, and they couldn't wait to capitalize on his misfortune once he was down. He just hoped he was ready to be brave when the trouble came.

Always keep in mind that we are dealing with others who want similar things in life. They'll do whatever it takes to gain an advantage. A person must keep his head held high and stay focused on his goals.

He watched and waited for trouble to show up and wondered if he would be disappointed. He felt an eager anticipation to fight back that he couldn't shake. Every word he said made him eagerly await a response. Were people lying, frightened, or was he looking for attention? He didn't know.

People in the city tried to take everything from him except the clothes on his back. In a moment of clarity, the kid thought about life and the many jobs he'd been given, only to have them taken away without reason. He wondered when his moment to shine would arrive. Was he the one with a problem, or did others experience the same heartache?

He finally concluded that the only way to make money and escape possible financial sabotage was to do anything he could to offer his quality services to people and create his own business.

No matter what he came up with, the trials would be similar. With the talents he acquired from a life of hands-on, real-world experience, he looked at work opportunities as temporary contracts until he could fund his own business. He refused to be frightened of doing his own thing, especially since working for others never worked out.

As he walked through the back streets of a neighboring community one night, an unknown stranger confronted the kid and asked, "Want a job?'

"Sure, Mister. I wouldn't mind the extra money."

"I want you to do me a favor first," the stranger said.

"What did you have in mind?"

"I want you to wake up at seven o'clock in the morning, finish your chores at the house, walk to the neighborhood market, and buy flowers. Then I want you to take them to the coffee shop.

"Look for a lady with yellow shoes. Walk to her table and ask if you can sit with her for a quick drink of water. If she gives permission, thank her, and hand her one of the flowers. If she rejects you, walk away and take the flowers home. If she accepts the flower, sit at the table, ask the waiter for a drink of water, take a couple sips, and walk home to give your mother a rest. If she rejects the flower, leave the bundle of them on the table and walk away.

"Got it, Kid?"

"OK, Mister. No problem."

The stranger handed the kid a piece of paper with his phone number on it.

"Call me after you finish."

"Thanks." The kid walked home and went to sleep.

Never take people's kindness for weakness. That attitude always returns in some way. Do what can be done to maintain quality relationships, but remember, at the end of the day, people take care of themselves first. Do what can be done for others, and hope for the best.

The kid woke up and followed the instructions. He finished morning chores and went to the market to buy flowers. On his way to the coffee shop, he saw someone sitting at the table with the lady wearing yellow shoes. Instead of walking over to her right away, he waited out of sight for the guy to leave.

When he did, the kid watched the lady finishing her drink and approached her.

"Can I sit at your table for a minute to grab a quick drink of water?"

"Sure. No problem," she replied.

He offered her one of the flowers, which she kindly accepted. He asked a waiter for water, drank a couple sips, and said, "Thank you," before walking away.

Neither one had anything to say to each other. The kid took the flowers home and put them in water, then he called the stranger.

Sometimes, it's OK to say nothing to people. One needs true peace among friends when hanging out. People don't have to say or do much to impress others. People either accept someone for who he is or reject him.

The stranger answered the phone but didn't speak.

"Hello?" the kid asked.

"Before you say anything, I have to let you know that the lady spoke highly of you," the man said.

"What do you mean?"

"That lady is my wife, and I wanted you to meet her."

"She was nice to me. I didn't say anything to her except, 'Hi,' and 'Good-bye.' Before I approached her, I saw her talking with someone. I waited out of sight until they finished talking, before I went over."

"Thank you. Would you like to meet for lunch to discuss a possible job?"

"Sure."

"Meet me at the coffee shop at one o'clock tomorrow."

"OK." The kid hung up.

Be sure to follow instructions and pay attention to detail. That will save a lot of heartache and extra work.

The kid met the stranger on time. While sitting at the table, the kid noticed the man he'd seen with the lady approaching.

"I need to visit the bathroom," the kid said, walking away.

While in the bathroom, he heard arguing and waited for the noise to calm down before he returned.

"What happened?" the kid asked.

"Not much." The stranger showed the kid a map. "Have you ever seen anything like this?"

"No." The kid changed the subject.

Both wanted answers, and neither accomplished their goal. When setting up meetings, have clear goals.

Talk broke out through the city, though most of it was speculation, curiosity, and rumors. People wondered what kind of map the two were talking about, and why had the kid left the table right before the argument.

When people hear about treasure, they want it. Given the opportunity, many will seize any opportunity to escape their struggles in the hope of something better. That was the nature of the world. People also love to gossip and discuss what they've overheard.

Everyone should be careful what he discusses in public and watch the kind of company he keeps. Not everyone is a good person who has the best intentions.

The stranger and the kid felt mixed emotions about discussing treasure map details in a crowd of unknown people, especially since such people may not wish to work together toward a similar goal. Being honest in dealings with others was a good idea.

They thanked each other for the chance to talk, shook hands, and walked off. They wanted to consider the situation before deciding if another meeting was wise.

Be careful not to rush into decisions. Take time to find out the best options and then make a responsible decision.

People should be given the chance they can be trusted. They should be given an opportunity to be responsible with a bit more, not too little. If they can be trusted, then give them even more. If they can't be trusted, take away their privileges. Many have genuine blueprints to treasure lying around for others to work toward. There are no secrets to success. All it takes is hard work, responsibility, honesty, and trust. Most of all, one most show integrity.

Have people ever been so angry at what they see in life that simple communication doesn't solve the problem? That's reality. We must stand in line at the complaint department along with everyone else and notice who listens. Not many, right? Exactly.

Ever since I can remember, I endured many trials, errors, and successes in pursuing a credible education and attempting to maintain income to provide for my family and create a life for myself. In the process, I learned many valuable lessons and went through many pains and challenges in life.

My goal is to offer assistance to help others accomplish something of value in their lives while creating a life for myself and my family of which I can be proud. I have many ambitions. One happens to be storytelling in the hope of leaving a lasting impression with those who take the time to read my work and pass on the messages or the lessons learned and appreciated.

Caught between a bad decision and an even worse one, the kid, who grew into a young man, wondered if he could escape judgment without minor collateral damage. Sitting in a courtroom, wearing a suit and tie, he couldn't seem to escape problems. He sat in a leather chair with his hands folded in his lap, awaiting advice from legal counsel. He more he heard, the more he felt he'd been framed. The options he was offered seemed like help and advice. People seemed to wonder, *when will the options we give him result in his ultimate downfall?*

He made better life choices than many in his situation. He worked many jobs and provided quality services any chance he could, but that didn't seem to matter to many people. What were they trying to accomplish that they couldn't just call him and talk to him about things?

His current court case was as unorthodox as his life. He wanted to spend time with people, but not in his present circumstances or within the options he was given. He noticed how people were and how they always offered conditional terms. What other people thought no longer mattered. In conversation with others, he heard many stories of similar failure and disappointment. He wondered what was next. Maybe it wasn't about him after all. Maybe he hadn't even done anything wrong.

As he wondered, court was called to order. The judge was ready to declare the sentence or charge the kid as not guilty. Suddenly, the young man fainted. He slipped from his chair to the floor. While others discussed what happened, he fell into a dream state.

He woke up in a bedroom at a construction site. After looking around for a minute, he walked into the bathroom to wash sleep from his face. When he looked at his reflection in the mirror, he saw everything around him was built from materials he bought. He had the feeling he was waiting for a decision to be made, but he didn't know from whom or when.

As he walked onto the construction site, he knew what he wanted to create, but he wasn't sure how to complete it. He sat in a chair on the patio that overlooked the land, closed his eyes, and, when he woke up, found himself in the courtroom again.

Picking himself up off the floor, he saw others getting up and trying to help him. He'd been out for a short time, but it felt like hours to him. The judge asked both attorneys if they would accept a quick recess to assess the situation. They agreed.

The young man thought that might be the time he needed to review his mental state. The stranger, who'd become a friend named French, was in court, awaiting the final decision. The attorneys and the judge decided to postpone the trial due to new evidence that arrived in support of O.

French and O developed a friendship over the years. French was a confidant and advisor in O's life. They talked often. Both had small circles of friends and didn't need much interaction with the general public. They walked quietly through society and didn't bother anyone.

That upset people for some reason, though neither one cared. They had friends and family and met occasionally to catch up on news.

After many nights of little rest and much contemplation about what to do next in life, O took another empty journal from his bookshelf and began writing. Over the years, he filled many journals of work that needed a bit of polish, but he had plenty of material to draw from as a storyteller. Some said he was a professional writer, based on what they claimed he'd gotten away with in life.

O met with French that night to discuss the trial and the possible new evidence that allowed him to return to work with new goals he'd recently written. He told French, "There's a story I want to write about childhood experiences I can't seem to shake. I didn't work with them while I was growing up.

"Some of the feelings and emotions in the story were factual, and some of it was exaggerated or made up, but I still relate strongly to the story. It should be a quality screenplay."

He began telling the story, starting with the logline.

"The son of an ex-agent audio records the murder of his family and an old friend. Two thieves break into the house, interrupting a game of Hide and Seek, stealing a map and a key from a safe before murdering the wrong family."

He began reading aloud while French listened.

Sitting under a streetlight on a highway, a kid wearing a hoodie has a backpack tucked under his right arm. A traveler drives down the highway and pulls up beside the kid. He gets out, lights a cigarette, and walks toward him.

"What happened, Kid? Why sit on the highway?"

"My family was shot and killed. I heard a gun go off while playing Hide and Seek with a friend. I heard feet shuffling, then the voices of two people giving instructions. After they took something from the safe in our house, they left. I stayed hidden until the house was quiet before going to see what happened."

"I'm sorry to hear that, Kid."

"That's OK, Mister. Life happens to everybody. Where were you going before you stopped?"

"A café to grab some breakfast. Are you hungry?"

"Sure. I know a place nearby."

They got in the car and drove away.

A car pulled up in front of a café-diner. The kid and the traveler got out and walked inside to a table, where the waitress brought them water.

"Want anything for breakfast?" she asked.

"Can you come back in five minutes?"

The kid wanted revenge and knew who to ask. The stranger was a gift, someone who might help fix the situation. The stuff in the safe was the key to a secret.

Without giving away the story, it could be classified as an action/adventure, mystery, or a crime saga. The story had twists and turns in relationships and several surprises.

By the time O finished reading, he and French shared a drink and then parted.

"Everything will be all right," French said. "Keep your chin up."

O hadn't spent time with a woman in a long time and decided to get a massage. He went to a place where he could get a back rub. The woman's scent was familiar, and her touch was firm and sensual.

As he lay face down, he couldn't help closing his eyes and re-memberingthe woman he spent time with and how he couldn't get very far with women who were kind, gentle, and loving.

After his massage, he walked home to sleep and prepare for an-other workday. He set out the paperwork he would need in a pile on his desk, showered, brushed his teeth, and slept.

When he awoke in the morning, he made coffee to start his day. While it brewed, he walked around the house, watering his plants and giving the cats their food and water. He took the laptop off the desk in his room and carried it to the coffee table in the living room to do some research.

He waited for a call about his upcoming court date and won-dered what the judge had decided, based on the new evidence.

CHAPTER 12

LITTLE TOKYO STORY

Michiko Tokunaga Kus

"Today it's Saturday, so we're going to *nihonjin machi* (Japanese town) to get some *nihon mo no* (Japanese items) and things we need," Mama said. "Papa wants to leave around eleven am, so we can get some lunch, too."

Oh, yum, I thought.

Papa drove, with Mama sitting in front and we three kids squashed in the back. It was a warm day, so the window was open. We got off the freeway and drove past Chinatown, and I looked at the pretty decorations on the Chinese shops and restaurants, almost like Christmas decorations.

We were almost at Little Tokyo when I felt dizzy, got carsick, and threw up. Everyone said, "Yeck!"

Mama cleaned me up. "You have to stay in the car, *fu no wa li* (embarrassing) with *ge ge* (vomit) on your blouse. Sit on the floor, so no one sees you."

Papa always walked us to Azusa Street, near the Japanese markets and stores where he and Mama shopped. He bowed his head to pray, saying, "This is where Grandpa came to help the evangelist, William J. Seymour, in the 1900s when he started the Azusa Street revivals."

Papa told us that Grandpa said his father came to America by boat in 1880. He was already a Christian. Their township in northern Japan had a memorial tomb for Jesus.

"But Papa," I asked, "why would Jesus go to Japan?"

"Why not? The Bible doesn't say anything about what he did after he taught at the temple at age twelve until he started his ministry in Israel at age thirty. After Jesus' resurrection and just before he went to Heaven, he told his disciples, 'Go into all the world and preach the Gospel to all creation.' Why is it hard to believe that He went into the world to preach the Gospel?

"In 1900, when Evangelist William J. Seymour started the Azusa Street Revival, your grandpa was part of the team of helpers: *hakujins* (Whites), *kuronbos* (Blacks), *nihonjins* (Japanese), and other Asian and Mexican Christians. That's why you were named William, after the evangelist."

"But Papa, Azusa Street is just a small alley."

He sighed. "I know, but there was a powerful Pentecostal revival there in the 1900s."

"Papa, maybe someday they'll put up a memorial statue for William J. Seymour. Why don't you do it?"

"Me? Hmmm."

"Maybe that reporter from the Japanese paper who wrote about Grandpa's hometown in Japan would help. Maybe we could put some nice benches to sit on and plants and flowers so butterflies and hummingbirds would like to come. You know the missionary who painted the pretty picture on the wall of our church? Maybe he could paint a mural on the wall in the alley, so people would know this is a very special place, not just another lonely alley."

"That sounds like a good idea."

"I'll ask my African-American friends at school if they know who William J. Seymour is. If they don't, maybe their church would help fix up Azusa Street. Let's pray that churches all over will want to help make this a special place to visit.

"There's a *hakujin* (Caucasian) lady from church named Williams, and she's a missionary to Japan. She helps start Christian churches and shares the Gospel with Japanese people. Do you think it's a holy coincidence that the Azusa Street evangelist was named William J. Seymour?

"In the Japanese newspaper, a reporter said he was given a copy of the Smithsonian history magazine with an article called, *Land of the Rising Sun.* the article said that Jesus of Nazareth, the Messiah, didn't die on the Cross of Calvary but died and was buried in Japan. Maybe the article should've been called *Land of the Rising Son.* In the Bible, Jesus was crucified on the cross, then He rose again on the third day.

"In my Sunday-school class, the teacher taught about the Gospel of Luke and how the thief on the cross beside Jesus asked Jesus to remember him when He reached heaven. Jesus told him, 'Today you will be with Me in paradise.' He said it's written that Christ will suffer and rise from the dead on the third day, and that repentance and forgiveness of sins will be preached in His name to all nations, beginning in Jerusalem."

"William," Papa replied, "people can be very stubborn., Keep praying for eyes and hearts to open."

"The teacher also said that in Exodus 14, the Lord told Moses, 'Quit praying and get the people moving.' H--ow can we get people moving for Azusa Street?"

"I don't know, Son," he said sadly.

After Papa took us to see Azusa Street, we went shopping. That usually took an hour. Usually, we ate lunch at a Japanese place. Today, I thought they would visit the only Chinese restaurant in Little Tokyo. They had the yummiest almond duck. Mama said I could eat boxed leftovers when we got home.

I sat in the car, glad it wasn't too warm.

Occasionally, I sat up to peek out the window at the people walking past carrying bags. Some had boxes probably filled with my favorite sweet *mochi* (Japanese pastry). Usually, Mama bought some, too.

Two men came to the car when the street was empty. Looking mean and sneaky, they glanced around a lot. Both men had their hands in their pockets. One man took out his hand and had something shiny in it. I was scared.

Then a tall, big man in a *hapi* coat (Japanese print jacket) came up to them. They turned and saw him, then they ran off.

The big man leaned down and smiled at me. "Don't worry. Your parents and brothers are almost finished shopping. Your Mama even bought you an *azuki* snow cone, your favorite."

I loved the flavor of sweet, crushed *azuki* beans.

I looked out the back window to see if they were coming, but they weren't. I turned back to the side window to ask the big man where he saw them, but he wasn't there. I watched a pretty white dove fly into the sky.

A few minutes later, Mama, Papa, and my brothers walked toward the car with many bags. Mama held a snow cone.

When they reached the car, she opened the door and handed me the *azuki* snow cone. She looked at me, surprised.

"How did you clean your blouse?" she asked. "It's not dirty with *ge ge* (vomit)."

I didn't tell them about the two mean men or the nice tall man in the *hapi*, because Mama and Papa might not let me come to see Little Tokyo again if strange men came around when I was alone.

Every time after that, though, whenever we visited Little Tokyo, I never threw up again. I never saw the big man again, either, but I often saw a pretty white dove flying near the car.

I wanted to get a *hapi* coat like the big man's to wear for *obon* dancing for Nisei Week, where Japanese men, women, and children danced down First Street. We had to attend dance classes for months to learn the steps and hand movements.

"Why don't you wear the silk kimono I brought from Japan?" Mama asked.

"It takes too long to put on, and it gets so hot. I can't eat *mochi* or snow cones or *sushi* when I wear it."

"OK, but nothing expensive."

The first store we visited had a *hapi* coat with the same design as the big man's, and it was on sale. Outside the store window, a pretty white dove flew off once I put on the coat. It had a small tear in it, so it was on sale for half price. Mama said she could fix it.

I wore that coat to the Nisei Week Obon Parade and danced beside Mama. Papa danced, too. He wore his own *hapi* coat.

My brothers stayed on the sidewalk and watched with Auntie Jane and Uncle Tosh and my two cousins. They weren't interested in dancing but wanted to see the carnival, play games, and eat goodies.

Papa had a vegetable stand in Little Tokyo before the war. He never discussed his time in the relocation camp. Mama talked only occasionally about how they took only two suitcases each. She put what little money she saved into a teddy bear and sewed it shut to hide it. On the train to Manzanar, the windows were painted black so she felt certain they would all be killed at the end, but then the soldiers handed out lunch boxes. She said the food didn't taste very good, but she was relieved, because if they were being fed, it didn't seem likely they would be killed.

After the war, when we left Manzanar, we lived in a small apartment building in Boyle Heights, just over the bridge from Little Tokyo. Then, we moved to a trailer park in Sun Valley. The trailer was so small, when we kids walked to one end, the other end lifted up. Mama yelled at us to stop it, but it was fun.

We moved to a small rental house in the San Fernando Valley. Mama and Papa finally saved enough money to buy a house a mile away. Since Mama didn't drive, we put everything into my little brother's wagon to move from our rental to our new home. It took a long time. Papa was at work gardening. After the war, many Japanese men gardened, because jobs were hard to find for "enemy aliens."

We lived near a high school, and Mama found a broken baseball bat one day. She sanded it down and used it to pound sweet rice to make homemade *mochi*. That was really good. My favorite was heating it on a metal grill on the stove until it was lightly brown and puffed up, then eat it with a *shoyu* (soy sauce) and sugar mix. To get the sweet rice, Papa had to take us to Little Tokyo, since they didn't sell that at regular markets. He also bought the *soba* (buckwheat) noodles for New Year's and supplies for the fancy *sushi* Mama made. Now we can get that at the Asian markets all over the valley. There was a little Japanese market in the valley, but it was more fun to go to Little Tokyo and get the yummy *mochi* and snow cones.

Recently, my friend, Mariko, gave me a ride to the Little Tokyo Library to hear a Japanese writer and take a walking tour of Little Tokyo. They said the Japanese American National Museum, JANM, frequently gave tours. She had to leave early for a family gathering, so I said I'd take the bus home. In the '70s, I rode the bus from the valley to go to Los Angeles to work, so I thought it would be interesting to see how it was then. I went to the Little Tokyo Service Center, and the lady told me which bus to take.

At the bus stop, I saw a homeless man sitting with a black bag of possessions. I had half my *bento* box (lunchbox) left, and I asked if he'd like it. I told him I hadn't eaten from it, just scooped some onto a plate. He accepted it.

The bus to the valley was five blocks away. I decided to walk rather than wait for a bus to take me there.

It was the first time in over forty years I took the bus. It was only twenty-five cents for seniors, but the driver didn't have change, so it cost me one dollar.

After I got off the bus in the valley, the lady waiting at the bus stop told me about the cost.

I sighed and said, "I guess it'll cost me another dollar to get home."

She laughed. "Here's a quarter."

"You don't have to do that."

She laughed again. "You shared your *mochi* (Japanese pastry) with me, so please accept the quarter."

It was still light when I left Little Tokyo, but I didn't get home until 7:30 PM. It was a long ride from Little Tokyo, but I had a mini-tour of Los Angeles to the valley.

CHAPTER 13

BETRAYAL FOR BEAUTY

William Lynes, MD

It was his day to confess, but as the sun rose, he longed for more time. His guilt, hatred, and self-loathing were so overwhelming, he couldn't stand to be alone any longer. Painful remorse plagued him since the incident, the sin he committed so overwhelming, even one more day of postponement was unbearable. The day to pay for his action was upon him, and he couldn't allow anything to postpone it.

Even before the servant roused him that morning, he lay awake on the finest silk bedding, realizing the tortuous morning had arrived. When he was alone again, he sat on the bedside with his head in his hands, his long red hair and beard disheveled from days of inattention, a sick feeling of revulsion in the pit of his stomach.

He looked across the room through the window, seeing the beautiful rising sun, and remembered for the first time in so long, God was there for him. He knelt on the cold stone floor, praying with words that were so easy in the past, though now it was painful with none of the usual endearing expressions coming to his lips. His pleas to God rang empty. His guilt was deep, but he knew God wouldn't abandon him. At times in the past, he danced for the Lord on those same stone floors, but the thought of doing so sickened him.

Servants worked for hours preparing a wood fire-warmed bath, and he cried as he soaked in the perfumed waters, remembering his triumphant life in ruin, as if smashed upon the shoreline boulders of the Jordan River. The army had stagnated for forty days in the valley of Elah, when as just a child, he slew the giant and cut off his head using only his sling and the giant's own sword. Faith in the God of Israel was his source of power. That faith protected him through years of angry pursuit by an insane King Saul and kept him from slaying the man when he was in his hands in the cave at En Gedi. He was a man of God's own heart, rich beyond belief, the master of all Israel and Judah. However, he had sinned against his Lord. Would God forgive him? Would he ever be able to live with himself again?

David tried to eat the bountiful breakfast laid out in his chamber. The servant left quietly, unaware of his master's anguish. David ate very little, because hunger wasn't the source of the sick feeling that plagued him in his stomach for so long. Turning to his harp, he tried to play, which was always a source of relief in the past, but it was as if the Lord wouldn't listen anymore.

He moved to the throne room and sat timidly. That throne, symbolic of his riches and kingdom, was a gift beyond imagination. As he sat, he felt the feeling come again, the one he felt for a long time—the throne was large, but he was just a small man, too small to occupy it anymore.

As he sat and waited, the words of the Prophet Nathan refused to leave him. Long before, David heard the parable, which was so ominous and so obviously intended for him, portending his demise so clearly, how could he not have anticipated it?

In the story was a man rich beyond belief, with possessions galore and many sheep in his herds. When faced with a feast, he took the sole ewe raised by a poor man for slaughter, rather than use one of his own flock.

When David first heard the story, he was furious, declaring the rich man should die, only to have Nathan said, "That man is you."

It later became obvious that he *was* that man, and he would finally confess his failure that day.

The manservant knocked gently on the chamber door before entering and saying, "Your queen awaits you, as you instructed."

David took a moment to straighten himself, looking in the mirror and wondering if he were strong enough. Dropping to his knees, he looked again to heaven and said a small prayer, hoping the Lord would forgive him and give him the strength to tell the woman of the terrible crime he committed.

Bathsheba was beautiful as always, one of his thirty queens. She was his favorite. She stood when he entered the room and kissed his hand, grateful as always for his presence, then she knelt before him.

"Master, you have summoned me to your chamber," she said. "What is it that King David wants of his devoted queen?"

David helped her stand and motioned for the servant to bring two chairs, so they could sit beside each other. Staring at his sandaled feet, he pushed his long red hair behind his ear.

Looking at her sadly, he said, "Bathsheba, I have sinned against my Lord and against you."

The woman touched his arm. "No, my king. You are loved by the Lord beyond any man, and I, too, love you."

David shook his head. "You don't know the truth. Not one more day must pass before I am honest with you."

She sat back, timidly waiting.

David looked into her eyes for a moment, then he stared at the floor, unable to maintain eye contact. Taking a deep breath, he began his story.

"In the spring, at the time when kings go off to war, I sent Joab, all the Israelite army, and your husband, Uriah the Hittite, against the Ammonites at the siege of Rabbah."

Bathsheba looked away at the mention of the man's name.

"I did not go myself to lead the army, as was my duty."

She looked at him with a questioning gaze.

"I sent for you after seeing you bathing that fateful day. You were so beautiful I was overwhelmed with lust. I lay with you, a woman wedded to one of my soldiers." He paused while looking at her.

Bathsheba looked down sorrowfully. Without looking at him, she said quietly, "You are the king. You may do what you want."

David touched her chin and raised her face. "No, I cannot. Adultery breaks a clear commandment of the Torah. It was wrong, but what I did after that is the sin I will never be forgiven. You became with child, and I attempted to cover it up. First, I called for Uriah the Hittite. I asked him to stay away from the war, thinking that he would lay with you, and your child would be raised by him as his own."

She lowered her head and began crying.

"But he was a good man and instead stayed by my side. My nefarious plan failed."

"He was such a good man," she sobbed.

David lifted her head again and looked into her eyes. "He was a good man, Bathsheba. He told me he couldn't go to his home, for the Ark and Israel's men were camped in tents, so he, too, would not go home but would rather sleep on the marble floors of my palace."

His voice shook, and he choked back a tear. "What I did next is an abomination. Bathsheba, you must understand this. I have to tell you of my great sin against God and you."

She began crying harder. "No. You couldn't have done that!"

He was silent for a moment, staring down, his red hair hanging around his face until he brushed it back. "Do you know what I am about to tell you?"

She nodded, tears running down her face. Her grief was inconsolable.

"I must tell you. It's more than I can stand on my soul. I ordered Joab to place Uriah the Hittite on the front line and for my men to fall back. The army obeyed. That is why Uriah is dead. I'm responsible for his brutal slaying."

"No!" She stood and pounded him with her fists. "I suspected, but in my wildest dreams, I didn't think it could actually be true." Her shoulder slumped, and she collapsed before him.

David was crying, too. He wiped his face, choking back tears, and looked at the queen before him. "Our son.... The Lord took the young boy born to us because of my evil."

She cried continuously for several minutes, and he let her. When she seemed done, he touched her shoulder and kissed her head. "Can you ever forgive me and be happy in my kingdom?"

She looked up at him and dried her eyes. After straightening her gown, she sat up. "You are my king and have done great evil, but it's in the eye of God you must seek forgiveness, not with your servant. I love you and will continue to be your queen."

While Bathsheba continued to be King David's devoted and favorite wife who forgave him, his kingdom and life would never be the same. Nathan had foretold that while David lived, his kingdom would always be at war, because those he loved would rebel against him.

What David did greatly displeased the Lord, but, unlike Saul, his predecessor, David repented. While he did great evil in the eyes of God, he was forgiven. David was a man after God's own heart, and his lineage would someday give rise to a true King, the Savior of the world.

CHAPTER 14

THE LITTLE TOWN

Heather P. Hardy

After being away for a while, I thought back to the little town in which I grew up and wondered, *Are towns meant to stay little?*

Everything was simple and complete, filled with people I met at school and at play. I had a feeling of belonging and a love of everything natural and good, but the little town that raised me wasn't where I stayed. When I grew up, I moved away. No matter where I lived, whether a little town or large city, I always remembered the feeling of being someone, a gift from the little town where I grew up. Perhaps the little towns we all grew up in made sure we would feel that way.

As I began my grown-up life as someone people thought of as famous, I often remembered that little town and how it helped me succeed. I had a strong belief in myself and a firm understanding of right and wrong. I carried a sense of self-respect and respect for others as part of my childhood, as did many people who grew up in little towns they love. As my life became more hectic, remembering those good feelings became more difficult.

Life was good, yet things happened at times. I lost my job. I had to become myself, so I sang. I did it so well, I became famous for it. After years of work, when I finally felt the need to retire, I remembered how my little town made me stronger in life. That strength helped me through the hard times.

Part of that strength came from friends and teachers and the fun I had with them and my family. The happiness we shared took away the tears during those hard times.

I often wonder what my little town looks like now. I took the time to travel back there. As I drove through, I noticed it all seemed quiet and the same. With all my heart and mind, I wished I could be young again and relive my years in that town.

I left the area and returned to where I currently lived --another little town. I realized I was happy there, as I'd been happy growing up. It came to me that some people live in towns that aren't that little, and they might have been more difficult to live in and grow up in. Times must have been harder for them, too.

When I returned home, I realized it was wrong to stay in my little-town memories. Other people needed more help than I did. I visited a larger town and saw there were many places I could help.

I found a way to help my neighbors by volunteering at the largest hospital in that town.

Then one day, I met someone. He came from my hometown, and we grew up together, going to school as children. He was a patient in the hospital where I worked. I looked at him in his hospital bed and saw he was very ill. Remembering him, I slowly went to his bedside.

We talked about our childhood fun. We both remembered being on a baseball team together. We laughed at the memory of being 10-10 in the final inning of the game. He hit a homerun to win the game for our side, and we took the title that year.

I left his room that night with a warm, good feeling. He smiled and said, "Thank you. I enjoyed our talk."

I returned to work the following day and found his room was empty. The staff at the nurses' station told me he died during the night.

I went to pay my respects to his family and to him at his funeral. Afterward, I sat alone, trying to collect my thoughts.

He lived as an adult in a larger town, yet we had our childhood and the little town we grew up in to remember. Lowering my head, I pressed my hands together. No matter what we'd been through, the little towns and larger towns gave us each other. I felt a sense of our lives together, a love of my country, and how good it was to live here.

Life has always been about being here and being human. Human feelings make towns more than just places to live. Our memories and feeling for each other intermingled and brought a spirit of love to us all. It was certainly true for me. I was thankful I had known him and told his family that.

Those towns remain firmly in place, just like people. They are filled with the beautiful memories of growing up in those towns we share, whether the towns are large or small. We are free to meet the challenges of our world in that way. All across our nation, towns large and small are full of life and beautiful memories of shared events and fun.

That day when I traveled in my mind, I learned how I cared for other people and how they cared for me. Traveling to those places gave me a beautiful gift.

EDITOR LARRY PARR has had hundreds of regional productions. Dramatist Guild and Sarasota Area Playwrights Society member. Awards include: HI-HAT HATTIE Kansas City's Drama Desk Award for Best Musical, Florida Individual Artist Recipient, American Cinema Foundation's First Prize for Screenwriting; MY CASTLE'S ROCKIN' Southern Appalachian Repertory Theatre's ScriptFest, first white playwright produced in the history of the National Black Theatre Festival; INVASION OF PRIVACY 1999 Gold Coast Players best-play award, The National Arts Club's Playwrights First Award in Manhattan, Ashland New Play Festival, Theatre Conspiracy's New Play Competition, Florida Individual Artist Recipient, and Dezart Performs Audience Favorite, Best Actresses, Beat Actor, Best Director, Best Supporting Actor, Best Supporting Actress in Palm Springs; SUNDEW Southern Appalachian Repertory Theater's Annual Play Competition, Judith Chapman Best Director Desert Theater League Awards; HIS EYE IS ON THE SPARROW Florida Individual Artist Recipient, The Sarasota County Arts Council's John Ringling Fellowship Grant, Daytony Award (Dayton's Tony Award) Best Overall Production; SHUNNED Southern Appalachian Repertory Theater's ScriptFest Winner, Utah Shakespeare Festival, New American Playwrights Project, Julie Harris Playwright Award Finalist. He was a winner of Florida Studio Theatre's Short Play Competition nine years in a row. He won STAGES '93, the 1994 Porter Fleming Playwriting Competition, The Arion Award For Music Excellence, Civic Recognition Award, and the Broome Agency's Best-Novel Award. In 2000, and in 2010, Florida Studio Theatre presented him with the Barbara Anton Playwriting Award. In 2002, he was chosen as a participant in The Floridian Project with a play about Harry T. Moore. He is the author of three published novels and the editor of hundreds of published books. www.larryparr.info

CPSIA information can be obtained
at www.ICGtesting.com
Printed in the USA
FSHW020637150421
80389FS

9 781892 986238